The Serpent

in the Garden

J E Rutherford

THE SERPENT IN THE GARDEN

First published by Lulu

2008

ISBN 978-1-4092-0023-9

Dedicated with gratitude to the memory of

Agatha Christie

J.E. RUTHERFORD

1
In the Rectory Garden

It was a glorious autumn day, the sky crisp and blue and the golden yellow-green beeches and oaks crowded with nuts. By mid-morning the frosts had cleared and it was cheerfully mild; and this is why the first body was discovered that day rather than remaining silently waiting for who knows how long. As it was, Angela Carrington, the Rector's wife, decided that this late opportunity to do a little more gardening was too good to miss. Wrapping herself up therefore in waxed jacket, hat and boots, she passed through the back door of the Georgian Rectory and across the yard to the outbuildings. She collected wheelbarrow, secateurs, pruning knife, saw and spade, before proceeding through the passage between the outbuildings, into the overgrown jungle she liked to refer to as 'the walled garden'. Here neglect had conspired with a sow and her piglets (the property of a previous occupant) and a few surreptitious bonfires, to create an exotic wilderness of clematis with trunks like tropical vines, brambles and nettles of an exaggerated scale, willow, sycamore, thistles of more varieties than she had known existed, and some valiant crocosmia. In the middle of it all was an unprepossessing mound of unburnable bonfire residue, within which she had previously recognised bedsprings, and at least part of a filing cabinet. As usual the sight deflated her optimism despite the weather; but she had visions of a pond, of yellow autumn-fruiting raspberries, of strawberries, and a bench where one could sketch or read or pray in dappled stillness. And so, in hopeful anticipation that sooner or later someone would notice her toil and volunteer a crew of gardeners and a digger, she began another bout of hacking through the worst of it all.

The sow had displaced most of the paving stones at the back of the outbuildings, but as willow and brambles were growing in the seams it hardly mattered; eventually they would all have to come up and the roots be dug out. She had settled for cutting things back to ground level and shovelling off the debris so that the outline of the paved area was clear, and it could be walked upon. Likewise, the shallow concrete pond that lurched drunkenly where the sow had left it, had been cleared out and awaited the heavy work of reinstatement or replacement. It was with a sinking heart that she realised that her efforts had brought her to the edge of the tangled mass of bonfire remains. In the manner in which one dips one's toe into a pool of uncertain temperature, she decided to cut back the brambles and nettles around the mass and attempt to remove some of their roots, and thus determine the extent of the rubbish heap before facing the task of clearing it.

It was in the midst of this activity that, energetically digging up a willow root, she found that her spade had revealed something she was sure she didn't want to see. With the unerring instinct we have in the presence of the genuinely appalling, she knew this.

So she sat down with her back to the hole to recover her breath before turning and looking at the oddly shaped thing that she was certain was a human finger. She was equally certain that it would reveal itself still to be attached to its hand, arm, etc. etc. 'I have found a body', she thought to herself, and the unbidden thought followed that this was exactly the sort of place where one might be expected to do such a thing.

She must go and get the police — but she ought not to leave the body unprotected from birds and animals. Fearful of disturbing evidence while aware that she must already have done so with her digging, she found a fertilizer bag and put it over the hole, weighting the edges with stones. She felt that she must have this sorted out before her husband Matthew came home; it seemed that somehow it would be her fault if he came home to find that there was a human body in his garden. She had reached the telephone; Who should she ring? She turned the pages looking for *Carabinieri* before cursing herself for a fool and turning instead to *Garda Síochána.* Why were the police only listed under stations, not usefully under departments, like 'homicide'? Why didn't every country have *Carabinieri*, or *Gendarmes*, easily contactable in emergencies? Their own local Garda station, she knew, was only manned part-time, and the larger station half an hour away wasn't much better. How to get the right person? Who would know? To this last question she at last found an answer. She lifted the receiver and dialled. 'Fr Enda is that you? It's Angela from the Rectory. Thank heavens I got you

in. I'm afraid something extremely serious has happened
— I can't speak on the phone but could you please wait
for me and I'll be down with you straight away. It really
couldn't be more important. Yes. Thank you so much.
I'll see you in a minute. Goodbye.'

'I am babbling. I am becoming hysterical' she
thought, with perfect detachment. The car bumped down
the Rectory drive and she peered out at the road — left
as far as the gatelodge of the Abbey, and right towards
the town. All clear. She pulled out and turned right,
passing the hurling club and the garage. Everything she
did seemed to her very slow and unhurried, with lots of
time in between to think and observe. 'Everything has
gone into slow-motion', she thought. 'I am hysterical.' It
took ages to pass the hurling pitch, and the bungalows
across from it. Then came the garage with its huge
agricultural tyre on display in front, then more
bungalows, and the new development opposite their
national school. She realised that there was a Garda
patrol car coming towards her. Should she stop and jump
out and wave them down? There would just be time. *Ma
non bisogna la polizia stradale!* And with the absurdity
of this thought the car had passed and the opportunity
was lost. She was both surprised and irritated with
herself that in this crisis she was reverting to being
Italian. The daughter of a Scottish Anglican priest and an
Italian Methodist (for there are such things), home had
always been the small Anglican chaplaincy in Arezzo,
though she had been sent to a girls' school in Scotland

before dividing her university time between St Andrews and Bologna. Fiercely proud of her father, when asked her nationality she always replied 'Scottish.' But now the only thing she found to say to herself as she drove along was *Mamma mia!*

By this point she had reached the town square and was facing the miraculously unspoilt centre of Ardliss. Around an irregularly shaped green were distributed two churches, two banks, two butchers, two news agents, a post office, a hardware store, an hotel, a bakery, a pharmacy and innumerable pubs, among other things. All this was approached by six roads. She edged cautiously out of hers and a few minutes more saw her safely ensconced in an armchair in the parochial house with a glass of mellow sherry, while Fr Enda, having swooped upon her crisis like a protective mother hen, made his telephone calls with the calm authority of one born locally, who knew and was known by everyone.

As she waited she clung to one certainty: in a rural community people don't go missing without it being noticed. The Church of Ireland parish indeed, though covering the geographical area of a small principality, with large chunks of two counties and a morsel of a third, numbered its flock in the low hundreds. The idea that one of their number had been murdered without being missed horrified her; but otherwise, why leave the body at the Rectory? Why leave a body at the Rectory in any case? And all the while the vision of the overgrown wilderness in the walled garden nagged at her.

THE SERPENT IN THE GARDEN

'Terrible, terrible', said Fr. Enda, filling her glass without her being aware. 'What an appalling thing to happen to you. I simply can't believe in Ardliss having a body found in it. And to think it must have been there all along since before you moved in; that would make it more than a year. I can't recall when that garden was last used — I suppose someone took their chance while the place was unoccupied, before the renovation. Terrible. Now when you have finished that I'll take you home and we'll wait for the Guards. I have been *promised* that they'll be there straight away.'

But here fate had conspired against them, for the phone rang, calling Fr. Enda to the emergency of someone still living but expected to die, who took precedence over the already dead. Angela, her calm recovered now that the authorities were informed, assured him that he mustn't worry on her account. 'As you yourself said, the Guards will be there soon. I must return to keep an eye on things, especially in case Matthew walks in unawares. Thank you so much for your help.'

'But I haven't done anything at all; you'll both come back when we all have a moment and I'll give you dinner, and we can talk about it all. At least we know that it can't have been anyone local, or we would know by now. There can't have been a murder here for eighty or ninety years. You can count on it that it will turn out to be some Dublin gangland killing, and they found the Rectory empty and neglected and took their chance.'

'I'm sure you're right, Father.' But as she drove home she brushed a wisp of hair out of hazel eyes that were troubled, for reasons she had not had time to explain to Enda.

So it was that Angela took her position beside the body and said what prayers she thought appropriate for the poor abused individual whose remains had ended up in her garden. Already her quick imagination saw the walled garden excavated and gone over with a fine-toothed comb. Sternly banishing the unbidden thought that she would finally be rid of the willow roots (and surely someone would have to move the bedsprings and filing cabinet), she realised that in future the garden would also be a memorial place for whoever it was whose body it now held. Suddenly she felt very strongly that some sort of rite ought to be undertaken in the garden after the removal of the body. She wondered absently what sort of Anglican rite there might be for such a thing; there must be something, she thought, because people do find bodies, if only infrequently. She remembered the old rite for the 'churching of women', a thanksgiving for safe delivery after childbirth. She had heard how it had once been adapted as a thanksgiving for someone's recovery after having been gored by a bull. But that rite wasn't in the new *Book of Common Prayer*, she felt sure.

While Angela mused her eyes strayed to the back wall of the garden, still overgrown with ash and willow and ivy, all of which would have to be removed to save the wall from final collapse. It was an old wall, like the house – Georgian, though the foundations of the wall might be older. Within the confines of the boundary wall the Rectory and its grounds bore the marks of generations of occupation. Immediately to Angela's right a broken gate led out of the walled garden to a disused lane that ran from the house to the main road. The lane must have been as old as the wall; along it tradesmen's vans would have delivered goods to the house. It was now very close to being an unrecoverable wilderness. Between this lane and the drive down which Angela had passed earlier was a tangled field that Angela had christened 'the meadow' — a romantic word for a ruined mess of ruts, formed when the grounds were being cleared of the worst of the overgrowth before the Carringtons moved in. Parishioners who had grown up in the vicinity of Ardliss remembered when there had been a tennis court at the bottom of the meadow. Tennis guests had arrived by the back lane and brought their bicycles to the court through an entrance in the lane wall cut specially to accommodate bicycle handles. Angela supposed that the bicycle-shaped entrance must still be there, under the sycamore and brambles. She could not imagine the meadow ever having been dry enough to play tennis on. Her first winter, realising that she would never get the meadow ploughed straight again, she had planted trees to make it a leafy wood: red and silver maple, walnut, bird cherries; nearest to the house some mespils around the ancient beech, and nearest the road golden willow to soak up the tidal waves that lorries sent over the wall in the winter. She knew that she would never see the wood in its maturity, but she enjoyed envisioning it, and hoped future residents would enjoy it.

The remnants of the avenue that had adorned the drive were also scrappy and in need of a serious overhaul. To the few mature beeches that remained, a previous occupant had added quick-growing conifers, too densely planted, and too near the beeches. At some point a lime had been felled and the stump allowed to sprout like a Medusa's head. In due course Angela would put all this right too. On the far side of the drive a hedge marked the Rectory field, three and a half acres which swept in front of the house and around the far side, where it bounded the ghosts of an orchard and a shrubbery. Angela thought of the lives that had been passed in this house: the cook/housekeeper taking deliveries through the yard into the back of the house and downstairs into the kitchen. A groom living beside the stables — now an open garage for her small car. Originally the Abbey's land agent had lived here, but when the old Rectory next to the church had burnt down, this house had been given to the parish, and it had been the Rectory ever since. Children running in the orchard, tennis parties, the Rector in his study, and after dinner with his family in the drawing room before the fire. Many families and many lives had passed in this house, yet Angela was unable to imagine any circumstances that would result in a body being buried in the garden. At the same time she knew that such reflections were merely idle.

THE SERPENT IN THE GARDEN

She shifted her gaze from the boundary wall to beyond it, through the sycamore and willow to the immaculate fields of Blandings. At this thought she stirred uneasily. The inhabited Abbey next door is not, of course, called Blandings; but Angela had developed the habit of thinking of it like that, so much so that she sometimes called it Blandings in conversation. She would not have done so on purpose; but benign, mildly eccentric peers always reminded her of Lord Emsworth. It is possible that the late departed Rectory sow also brought the Empress of Blandings to mind. In any case, the habit of calling the abbey 'Blandings' had now spread among those parishioners sufficiently acquainted with P.G. Wodehouse to see the joke. She hoped that William and Helena hadn't heard it, because the allusion would certainly not be lost on them. Here she reflected how sensible it was of William and Helena to have themselves referred to locally simply by their Christian names, or as Mr and Mrs Chancellor. It must have saved a year of communal time, as well as sparing themselves being referred to by any number of imaginative variations on their proper titles.

At this point the Guards arrived, and proved to be the occupants of the very car she had passed earlier. 'Hello, this is the Rectory is it? We hear you've had some trouble', said one.

'It's here', she said, bringing them into the garden and indicating the fertilizer bag. She reached down to remove the stones, but they protested and told her not to trouble herself, this was their job. So she stood back gratefully while they lifted the bag and looked in the hole.

'Now, I wonder what this is? It might just be some sacking.' Angela was suddenly indignant, feeling like a child whose science experiment has been pronounced a failure by her teacher. But then 'No; we'd better get someone to look at this.' And turning to her the senior Guard said, 'Now don't you stay out in this cold; we'll take care of this. You go and make yourself a cup of tea, and don't worry.'

'I'll be inside when you need me', she said gratefully, becoming aware that she was indeed shivering in spite of the mild weather.

'That's right; in a little while we'll just ask you a few questions. But don't you worry about it now.'

Somehow tea did not seem adequate to the circumstances, so it was with a glass of Brunello that Angela sat in her studio and pondered that still-nagging question. It was not her problem. The professionals would deal with it. Once the body was away it would have nothing to do with them at all. But the fact drummed incessantly in her head: The body found under the willow, brambles, and nettles, under the bedsprings and filing cabinet, was not a skeleton. It was not even in an advanced state of decomposition. She very much doubted it had been dead more than a day or two. How on earth does one bury a body under so much rubbish and growth without leaving any trace? She found no answer to this question, so to calm her mind Angela did the only thing that she knew would absorb her thoughts.

THE SERPENT IN THE GARDEN

She sat down at her desk and began a very detailed drawing of Vermeer's 'Kitchen Maid'.

J.E. RUTHERFORD

2
Dramatis Personae

The reason I can tell you this much of Angela's thought processes is not because I am clairvoyant (as the authors of some novels seem to consider themselves), but simply because she herself related them to me. Everyone came round to me, one at a time, to give me their accounts of events as they had experienced them, so that I could write up the whole affair. Angela was one of the first, curled up on the sofa with a cup of strong Assam tea, looking out my sitting room window at the cutting-flower garden of 'Blandings'. I have lived in the outer-courtyard east apartment of Blandings for nearly twenty years now, and I fully anticipate retiring here and, in due course, dying here, if not in the nursing home-*cum*-clinic up the road at Drum. It was Penny, who runs the Blandings coffee shop, who first put it to me that I should write up an account of the murders. There was a general feeling locally that someone ought to; I would like to say that this was because we were all afraid of inaccurate and exaggerated reports being circulated in the press. But in fact, to be honest, the murders were the only interesting things to happen locally for more than a hundred years, and we confidently anticipate (and hope) that nothing much will happen to write about in the next hundred. This is our local saga, and it is felt that it deserves to be immortalised in print. It will certainly live for decades over our kitchen and dining tables.

15

THE SERPENT IN THE GARDEN

Admittedly, there was some concern at first that a published account would bring unwanted tourism to Blandings. We haven't the facilities needed to cope with more than one coach at a time, and it isn't as if we have anything like a safari park to make money out of lots of visitors. But the worst had already been done by the press. One murder might pass without much comment, but two gets you top spot on the evening news.

As it was, little by little we all began to realise that several of our number were starting to attempt writing the story; we ran the risk of seeing some dozen rival versions all hitting the publishers at the same time, and ending up in a muddle that satisfied no one. For all our faults, those of us who have lived here forever, and whose families have lived here forever, are only still here (and have not murdered each other before now) because we have a finely developed instinct for not stepping on one another's toes. It became obvious to everyone that there should be just one account, but that everyone should be able to report his or her 'evidence' to the writer.

As I say, it was Penny who put it to me that said writer should be me; I had not been one of the dozen or so original starters, so I was a bit surprised. But she said I would be suitable, because I had already written a book. I pointed out to her that what I had actually done was to make an edition of the Greek texts of the sermons of a fifth century bishop; these had been published in a volume together with my translation and commentary. This hardly equipped me for the writing of what was, in effect, a novel. But she said it was still a book, and besides I 'published things' (meaning that I had articles in print). I forbore countering that our very own 'Lord Emsworth' (let the reader understand) has written several books. For one thing, I didn't see that an entomologist was any better equipped to write up murder mysteries than a Patristics scholar. For another, William has far more important (and dignified) things to do, being a scholar of note; and he was in any case absent during most of the events to be told, on various bug-hunting safaris. I also forbore mentioning that Helena had also written a highly respected biography of Sheridan Lefanu; this seemed perilously near to constituting a 'transferable skill', and I knew it would be unfair to our long-suffering *châtelaine* to burden her with any more tasks than she already undertakes. The upshot was that, not having been one of the original authorial pretenders, and being perceived as neutral, it was agreed that I should write our official local account of the murders. And so they all came to me, as I have said, one by one, some excited and loquacious, others (like poor dear Angela) as to a therapist. I had the impression that Angela was unaccustomed to being listened to for extended periods, and felt rather guilty for taking my time. However that might be, she certainly did present me afterwards with a lovely portrait of my Abyssinian cat, Theophrastes.

I should also mention that the other thing that made me suitable for the task was the fact of my residence at Blandings. Not to beat about the bush (I fear I really am unsuited to sustaining mysteries), the puzzle of Michael Slattery's appearance under a pile of rubbish in the Rectory garden was soon explained. On the edge of a field at the extremity of the Blandings estate, bordering on the Rectory garden, an old disused drain was discovered which ran from the Rectory, under the walled garden (serving the defunct concrete pond in the process), then under the Blandings boundary wall. It was on the Blandings side that Guards found the manhole into which the body had been inserted. It had obviously been pushed as far along the drain as possible; the destruction of the pond in the walled garden, and general silting up of the drain had brought the body to a halt, purely coincidentally, under the rubbish heap where Angela was digging that day. So the first thing that brought Blandings into the frame was that the body had been deposited down that manhole. But the second, and far more important, factor, was that Michael Slattery had long lived on the Blandings estate in a converted barn, together with his wife, several small sons (I never have succeeded in counting them, they dart about so quickly), and an even greater number of Cocker Spaniels.

The shock of Michael's discovery was great, as you can imagine. At first no one thought much about who might be the culprit, only of Michael's widow and children, and the funeral. I'm afraid Fr Enda had a bit of unwanted media attention at the funeral, but he carried things off with his usual aplomb. Poor Sinead, the widow, was shielded from photographers by indignant mourners. It would not be an exaggeration to say that the entire town came to a halt for the funeral mass, which had to be broadcast outdoors by loudspeaker. This was not due to callous sensation-mongering. There was a very real shock and profound outrage that someone local had had his head bashed in, and had then been disposed of in such a barbaric way. And so the funeral reception was barely over before everyone began asking themselves 'Who?' and 'Why?' The 'why' seemed obvious to start with. It was received wisdom that Michael Slattery did shady deals. Granted, no one could itemise any, but it was 'known' that he had dodgy connections. What was certainly true was that he did very shrewd deals, which often left a sting after them. But if everyone of that description in rural Ireland were murdered for it, we would be living in a state of depopulated civil disorder. So that was as far as we could go, and it had to be left to the Guards to sift through Michael's acquaintance, personal and business, to try to make any more sense of it. We all attempted to convince ourselves that the crime would be traced to Dublin, where Michael had run an antiques business. But that manhole stood silently (as it were) accusing us: it spoke of local knowledge. The drain under the Rectory garden ran logically, if not literally, straight to Blandings.

Now in the normal course of things it wouldn't be difficult for the Guards to interview the residents of an estate and form some opinion of them as likely suspects. But Blandings is a complicated place. For one thing, it is geographically intricate. The boundary wall between the Rectory and Blandings runs from the Ardliss road, beside and then round the back of the

Rectory glebe, continuing towards Ardliss, running a fair way towards the town. This part of the estate, which borders on the Rectory, is devoted almost entirely to arable crops, wheat and barley. But as it nears Ardliss the estate wall has fallen into disrepair, and fields give place to an extensive plantation of cultivated softwood. Through this dense and dark evergreen forest runs a muddy farm track that never receives the full sun. This track eventually emerges onto the Rathcoole road, south-west of Ardliss. Beyond the wood, the estate turns into meadows for its large dairy herd, as well as the offices, sheds and enclosures of the dairy farm. Beyond the dairy farm I don't know how far the estate extends, and can only suppose that it is finally bounded by another wall beyond the dairy farm.

The park and Abbey thus lie beyond the Rectory, and are bounded in their turn by the park wall, which in places is also the estate wall. The north wall runs from the Rectory, along the Ardliss road and past the Abbey's main gatelodge on towards Drum for a bit, before turning sharply south and skirting the western side of the park. Turning left again, it passes the offices, barns and other buildings of the arable farm before reaching the forest, where the farm road loses its paving and becomes the forest track mentioned above. Among the cluster of buildings just before this wood is a small group of stone houses, originally doubtless built for estate workers. Two of these were occupied by the farm manager and the principal cowman, Billy, who is from New Zealand. But the others are let; and it was in one of these houses that Michael Slattery had lived.

I have given this description not in the hope that you will remember it, or even necessarily make sense of it, but in order to convey the higgledy-piggledy manner in which the different parts of the estate connect up. Like most working estates that have evolved over centuries, it is an irregular shape, comprising features that don't relate to one another, and indeed cannot easily be reached from one another. For example, there is no direct way to walk, let alone drive a vehicle, from the manhole by the Rectory, where Michael was deposited, to Michael's house. One is faced with extensive fields of plough, which at the time of his murder were planted in wheat. There is no path crossing these fields, and circumnavigating their boundary in either direction would take a couple of hours. Even if one walked across the fields towards Michael's house, progress would be blocked on the far side. To the west there is the garden wall of the Abbey itself, and to the south an embankment marking the edge of the forest, which is so deep and full of brambles as to be nearly impenetrable. Even if one were to beat one's way through to the forest path and turn west towards the farm and the houses, there would still be the muddy, rutted forest track to contend with, before one could arrive at last at Michael's house, a bedraggled and exhausted wreck.

Fields, forest, dairy farm, and park are all therefore effectively separate things, linked in ways probably known only to the employees of the estate. For those who come to walk in the park, and even for most of us who have apartments in the Abbey, wandering out of the park is disorientating and confusing. Sooner or later one seeks the inner wall, and the safety of the park. Entering the park through the back gate, off the lane where Michael had lived, the road divides in two, one part continuing ahead, up a rise, with parkland opening up on either side, the other sweeping around to the right and curving on to the front of the Abbey. Walking down either road one has a lovely view of the Abbey, as well as the sweep of the roads. After passing before the Abbey gate the right-hand road rejoins the left, and combined they then pass over a cattle grid, along an avenue of old oak and beeches, arable land to the right and grazing to the left, until after a mile or so one reaches the main gate and the Ardliss road.

The Abbey itself constitutes the other complicating feature of Blandings. In order to keep it, the gate lodges and cottages on the estate warm, dry and inhabited, Helena has devoted a great deal of time to converting every available space into self-contained flats and apartments, and every habitable building and room on the estate is tenanted. I have, as I have mentioned, lived here nearly twenty years, and I'm still not certain that I know of all the dwellings there are, or all their inhabitants. And indeed although I have stated that every possible space is inhabited, the truth is that every year or two Helena thinks of some ingenious way of devising new dwellings; barns and outbuildings, even a folly have been turned into human habitations. I suspect that only

J.E. RUTHERFORD

Helena knows the exact number of her tenants, and that even she would have to refer to her books to refresh her memory of them all. The Guards were therefore confronted not only with a confusing geography (which for all its complexities has only two entrances by road, and is almost entirely enclosed by walls), but also with a vast number of potential witnesses, and even suspects, to interview.

The effect that all this police attention had on us was the paradoxical one of making us collectively defensive, on the one hand, and mutually suspicious on the other. We instinctively closed ranks under the threat from 'outside'. But at the same time we tended to feel that there was little possibility that no one among us was involved in any way in Michael's murder, or at least had some knowledge of it. Grasping this nettle firmly, Helena sensibly convened a meeting of everyone resident on the estate, both tenants and employees. We were all asked to assemble for tea in the Great Hall, which was made as comfortable as possible despite its high vaulted ceiling and stone floor. As Penny boiled water and set out cups and saucers brought over from the tea room, faces familiar and unfamiliar began to appear. Soon a rather festive atmosphere developed, notwithstanding the circumstances. Introductions were made, and fellow residents discovered each other for the first time, or greeted one another as long lost friends. It must be said that the geographical extent of the estate coupled with the relative age of the tenants combined to inhibit even good friends from visiting each other as regularly as they might have liked. The elderly flocked together with glad halloos, and sat in chattering groups enjoying their tea with a relish peculiar to their generation. Of course, no one could seriously think that any of them were involved in the murder, and so they tended to regard the gathering as something of a treat. Those of us who can still consider ourselves (if only just) to be middle-aged, greeted one another in rather more sombre tones, and discussed the circumstances of our gathering mutedly, in groups of two or three. Yet, although our age did not prevent us from being considered as potential suspects, there is still the knowledge in middle age that one has already had quite a good life, and that there is only a quiet retirement to look forward to. So I suppose that really we were able to take some enjoyment in the novelty of the situation in which we found ourselves. It was the young who had my greatest sympathy. With careers and fortunes still to be made, brushing up against a serious crime is potentially most dangerous to them. And yet at that age there is still optimism, and a red-blooded thrill in any excitement. So as Max, the farm manager, arrived riding pillion on Billy's quad bike, they joined in a conversation that was nearly as animated as that of the elderly, though more nervous.

I have described our assembly in terms of age groups, because that was how we ended up organising ourselves. Other ties and similarities seemed less important somehow. Those in their twenties and thirties stood about together, many eschewing tea altogether. I remember the odd sight of Billy and Max talking to little Debbie English, who used to teach art in Galway, and Dr Claudia Crespi, an eminent herpetologist visiting from Rome. I myself was chatting to Penny as she served tea (much more efficiently than one would think given her arthritis), when I saw Mark Charles standing awkwardly on his own. Dressed as usual in flannels and sports jacket, he ran his hand through his fair hair and gave me a rueful, worried smile as he caught my eye. I had a suspicion then of what had happened; being an art historian with a particular interest in furniture, I supposed that someone had been hinting at some dodgy dealing between him and Michael on the antiques front. Taking a cup of tea to him I discovered that my supposition had been correct. 'It's damned awkward', he said. 'People think it's just harmless speculation, but it's actually very damaging to one's professional reputation. Ironically I'm more upset at being suspected of illegal trading than of being involved in a murder. That suspicion is merely ridiculous, but rumours of dealing in antiques could do me serious damage.'

At this point Helena approached the small podium of the Great Hall, and we realised that she intended to address us. We all moved to take seats. I noticed Cosmas and Maria Avakian, who are language teachers, encouraging the older generation to stop gossiping and to pay attention. Everyone seemed to want to be close enough to hear without being conspicuous to everyone else, and there was rather a scrum for the chairs in the middle. I found myself seated incongrously between Richard 'Dickie' Bird, a florid, balding property developer, and Mr Moto, an enthusiast of all things western, and especially megalithic or mediaeval. I will not try to replicate Mr Moto's English pronunciation. For one thing, it would be tedious to do so. For another, it seems to me that a people with such an abysmal record for learning foreign languages as we are, has no business ridiculing those who command a workable amount of English, especially when they come from such a very different culture. As I sat down I wondered whether Mr. Moto would have any trouble understanding proceedings. But he put my mind at rest. Wiping his glasses he gave me a smile and a little bow, and said, 'Thank you very much; I understand very well, better than I speak. Also I have heard much about this terrible thing, from many people.' I had no doubt that he had! I suppose that gossiping is one way to dissipate nervous tension. I began to detect within myself a greater degree of nervous anxiety than I had indeed been willing to credit. I took from my pocket my small meerschaum pipe (a little eccentricity that everyone humours), and with trembling fingers filled the bowl and lit it as I sat down.

By now, Helena was ready to speak. As usual she was brief and to the point. Drawing herself up to the full of her diminutive stature, she brushed a strand of greying hair from her penetrating blue eyes and began. 'Thank you all for coming this afternoon. I won't keep you from your tea for long, but I think we all need to be clear about the consequences of Michael's murder. You have all been very kind to Sinead and the boys, and I have obviously not asked them to be here today. You are no doubt aware that the Guards are at present among us, and will be asking everyone whatever questions they feel necessary to solve this crime. I must inform you that at present they have *no idea* who was responsible, or why the crime was committed. We must all therefore be extremely careful to refrain from speculation that could damage the reputations of innocent people, and cause ill feeling amongst us. When there are any developments everybody will be informed, but in the meantime we must get on as normally as possible, while giving the Guards whatever assistance we can.'

    As Helena continued, it occurred to me that it would be much easier to assent to such sensible advice than to put it into practice. Looking around me it seemed incredible that we were all embroiled in a murder investigation, and to judge from the expressions on other faces, I wasn't the only one for whom the whole thing still seemed unreal. If anything, Helena's calm good sense only added to the dreamlike quality of events. But even so, I had no doubt that this strange, numb state would not last long. And indeed, within a very short time we were all to discover how very real circumstances were, as the atmosphere at Blandings became increasingly electric.

3
The Victim

In addition to the mutual suspicion and sense of anxiety that built up in the Blandings community during that first police inquiry, there was the added drama of the enigmatic character of the victim. It would be pleasant to be able to say that Michael Slattery's violent death was the subject of deep grief and general mourning among the denizens of Blandings. But it would be, at best, an exaggeration. While revolted by the circumstances of his death, the inhabitants of the estate could not be said to have hung the flag (metaphorically speaking) at half-mast. There was something about Michael that made people uneasy in his presence. Charming, softly spoken and affable, he was never known to raise his voice in anger. But there hung about him the odour of plans and schemes, and there was something disquietingly calculated about his manner. The fact that nothing concretely criminal was ever laid at his door only heightened one's unease. You were sure he was up to something, but could never identify it, let alone prove it. And so he lent rather a *frisson* to what would otherwise have been a relaxed and tranquil existence among us. Those of us who live in apartments in the Abbey courtyards often have business in the house itself, whether helping with preparations for public events or receptions, or leaving cuttings, or borrowing cups of sugar, as it were. It was not an uncommon experience when in the house to encounter Michael emerging from a door in the panelling with a cheerful hello; he would pass on without any explanation, leaving behind a sense that he might be anywhere at any time, doing who knows what. When there were paying events at the Abbey those on the door found themselves checking furtively to see whether Michael hadn't entered by a side door without paying. I am not aware that he ever did so, but he had a way of making people suspect that he might do. Sometimes, entering a shop in Ardliss, one would find Michael speaking to the proprietor, and conversation would cease as one entered; this not infrequently coincided with the day of some big race or other sporting event.

To illustrate the effect he had on people I can cite an instance when he roused the suspicions of so open and trusting a person as Angela Carrington. It was at a sherry reception at Blandings. Michael seemed much taken with a young artist who (I was told) was making a name for himself in Dublin. I was standing with Angela when we overheard Michael telling this fellow that he believed he had acquired a painting in a country sale which was actually a *Fragonard* (I believe that was the name). At this I saw Angela's eyes widen with a contemptuous expression that I took to indicate her scepticism about such a possibility, or that she had indeed seen the painting and knew it to be something else. It is of course true that we all become a bit prickly when we hear other people claiming knowledge of our own pet subject. But I had never before seen Angela exhibit so much suspicion and curiosity, and that is what made the event stick in my mind. For the rest of the party she orbited the conversations Michael was having with his young friend, and indeed introduced herself to the visitor — a thing that I am sure she was not brought up to do, and which seemed quite out of character. When I subsequently found myself next to her again, she was gazing after them and she said: 'I wonder what he wants from that fellow?' I asked her what she meant, and she replied that she wasn't sure herself, and not to mind.

I have made these comments in order to give some indication of the sort of *ambience* that surrounded Michael. They might sound overly dramatic, but they give a good indication of how it felt to be around him. Michael really might have walked out of the pages of a novel by J. P. Donleavy. In fact, Matthew Carrington, our Rector, always suspected that Michael had consciously cultivated that image, and that he revelled in the mystery he created, without actually being any more than a sharp businessman. But then clergy are expected to see the best in people. Having said that, I must make it clear that Michael and I were not bosom friends. I am a straight-talking sort of person, and when the vapours of his mysteries became too opaque I was inclined to lose patience, and ask him 'But what exactly does it boil down to' type questions, which spoilt his effect. He retaliated by referring to me in public as 'Major', knowing that this is something I particularly dislike. It is embarrassing, and makes people turn and stare at me. He knew perfectly well that I had merely held a short-service commission in the Educational Corps — a folly I embarked on as a young academic facing the future with no family, having only a small inheritance and a doctorate on the Christian Platonists of Alexandria. I used to retaliate in kind by smiling sweetly at him whenever he did this sort of thing.

Given this state of affairs, discussion of the murder was even more defensive and uncomfortable in the Abbey than it was in any case bound to be. It seemed impossible to posit any credible motive for the crime that didn't seem somehow to carry an implicit criticism of the victim. It was equally difficult to exclaim how essential an addition to our society he had been, or how much he would be missed. If anything, getting himself murdered could be said to have been just like him — achieving an apogee of mystery and going out, as it were, with a bang. Only Helena, who has firm views on the presumption of innocence, and is never willing to believe ill of anyone until it is actually proved, was able to exclaim freely and without hypocrisy how dreadfully he would be missed. Her indignation on behalf of Sinead and the children was however universally and unstintingly shared, and we would all have risen up as a man, as it were, to help them in any way we were able, had that been required. But Sinead carried herself with great dignity, and apart from a few close friends, did not indicate a need for any assistance apart from the kindness to which any bereaved person is entitled. None of Michael's financial affairs became public, but after a while it became clear that

THE SERPENT IN THE GARDEN

Sinead had no major worries. She very soon took over management of the antiques business in Dublin, and life for the family proceeded, as far as we could see, as normally as could be expected.

And so, since other aspects of the murder were sensitive in one way or another, we became increasingly inclined to speculate about the mechanics of it: not the 'who', or the 'why', but the 'how', and 'where'. I am never sure how forensic pathologists know these things, but it seemed that Michael had not been murdered in the environs of the manhole. It was a source of growing irritation to Max, the farm manager, that the Guards had trampled so much of the field looking around, and that they had spent so many hours interviewing his men and asking them to show them round the farm. At first they seemed to think Michael might have been murdered near his house; so they tramped back and forth across the fields that formed the likeliest route from it to the manhole. This of course yielded no results, for the reasons I have given. So they then turned to looking along the wall between the Abbey and the Rectory, from the manhole to the main road. We could all have told them that no one would choose to drag a body over the boundary wall from the road, where there wasn't enough of a verge to stand on. Having said that, there were obviously not signs of disturbance in the wheat (at least until the arrival of the police!). The mystery of 'the body under the rubbish heap' was thus superseded by the mystery of 'the body with no visible means of arrival'. To my mind, that suggested that Michael was murdered beside the manhole, perhaps having made an appointment to meet someone there. But for reasons best known to themselves the Guards did not think so. Whatever evidence they had, led them to explore other avenues.

Police activity was becoming rather a spectator sport for us all when all of a sudden it became less amusing and much more alarming: in the middle of the morning one Wednesday they arrived at the Abbey. We had all been rather disappointed that they had only made one cursory visit before, asking if anyone had seen anything. But now here they were, cordoning off store-rooms, and taking a list of all occupants and employees. Suddenly we were in the midst of a very real police drama, much as they are depicted on television. One by one we were each interviewed; and not all of the questions were pleasant. It seemed clear that they were looking for motives among us, and for material evidence in the courtyards and outbuidings — presumably the murder weapon. So far their investigations had focused on Michael's house rather than the Abbey, so we were all rather shaken. Helena with her usual good sense gathered all the courtyard inhabitants into the library for sherry, to commiserate and compare notes. Little Mr Moto came in with his camera round his neck, flushed with successful ruin-hunting. The Avakians were there ahead of me, gentle and smiling as ever. It was difficult to imagine such modest and kind people having originated from a country with as violent a history as Armenia; they seemed ideally suited to the teaching of

THE SERPENT IN THE GARDEN

English to our many central European immigrants, which they undertook with great dedication.

I had just taken my sherry to the fire when my dear friend Catherine came in, moving painfully as a result of surgery on her knee. She lifted her glass and with a smile came to join me. Despite her white hair and dicky leg, it is easy to see the girl and young woman that Catherine was. Her rosy cheeks and frank smile, lit up by her sparkling blue eyes, are a tonic in themselves. Quite literally at times, since we frequently encountered one another over the tonic water in our favourite supermarket.

'How are you, Cathy dear?' I asked. 'How's the knee holding up?'

'Oh, don't ask', she replied, rolling her eyes. 'I seem to spend forever at the physio in Drum, and progress is so slow. I thought physiotherapists were supposed to manipulate joints and knead you like dough, but this one assigns courses of exercises, and seems to specialize in contraptions and machines. Every time I go she has something new to strap me into or plug onto me. I can't see that I notice it doing much for me, but there you are. I suppose it comes from being American. They always seem so fond of gadgets.'

'Yes, so I've heard. Apparently Matthew Carrington has a machine that stretches his neck, which he discovered through her. Still', I said, 'I understand you've got a new contraption yourself. Helena has been enthusing about your all-singing, all-dancing compost maker. I'd love to see it sometime.'

'Oh you must, do. Come round for a drink sometime and I'll take you out and show it to you. It's actually like a gigantic stomach; it digests organic matter in no time. The installation was a saga in itself. It's quite heavy, so it took them awhile to work out where they could put it. Helena is wonderful really to let me have it, since I don't think it would be easy to take it away again! I believe that there are only two others like it in Ireland.'

'Is it really true that you can compost animal droppings in it as well as vegetable matter?'

'Oh yes, that's the wonderful thing. It's hermetically sealed, and the internal temperature breaks down everything. It kills weed seeds, and any organisms that might be living in dung, so you can put everything in. You could scrape out your pots and pans into it.'

Cathy is the custodian of the Abbey's flower and vegetable gardens and supervises work in them, so composting is dear to her heart. She had long wanted something that would compost weeds and animal droppings, particularly given the proximity of the Chancellors' pet llamas to the vegetable garden. But at this fascinating point in our conversation our attention was caught by the appearance of Dickie Bird, an old friend and one-time beau of Cathy's.

'Oh, hello Dickie', Cathy said turning to him. 'I was surprised to see you the other day at the tea party; I thought you were away.'

'Yes, I had been;' he replied, coming up to us with a twinkle in his eye and a tug at his moustache. 'I only got back the day of the funeral to discover all the hoo-ha.'

'Where were you this time?'

'Out east. Thinking of investing in a little holiday complex in the Pacific. Not sure though. I've actually got plenty to do here, juggling with a few bits and pieces I picked up before the market hotted up.'

Not being as friendly with Dickie as Cathy was, this prickled me a bit. There is something about property speculation that I dislike; it so often raises prices beyond the means of people needing to buy a home for themselves. I was particularly annoyed however because it had only recently come to my attention that Dickie had bought the last remaining large field within the boundaries of Ardliss, and had received planning permission for over a hundred houses to be built in it. Our road infrastructure couldn't cope with a hundred extra commuters emerging into town every morning, and returning every evening. Besides, the land is very boggy, and I can't imagine it is really suitable for building.

'Are you still planning to have Bob Macnamee start building beside the school?' I asked; Bob being our local builder, and something of a property developer in his own right.

'Well, you know, I'm not really sure. There's such a glut of new housing nearer to Dublin, and much of it is still unsold. I'm biding my time and thinking about it. In the meantime I'm letting it for grazing.'

That, at least, was good news. I left Cathy and Dickie and turned to say hello to Penny, for once relieved of her tea-pot and apron. She was wearing a black dress and pearls, and seemed to regard the event as a party; and indeed why not make the most of our opportunities while we may? The tea shop was now shut up for the winter, there was a blazing fire in the library, and Mark Charles had been invited to play the piano. As he moved effortlessly from Chopin to Brahms he chatted happily in Italian to Claudia Crespi, who also seemed to have caught something of a party spirit. She had exchanged her waxed jacket, gumboots and *chignon* for a beautifully tailored little black dress, her luxuriant auburn hair for once allowed to fall freely about her shoulders. I must say it all made for a very cozy scene. By some symbiotic coincidence, Dickie and I both started fidgeting in our pockets at the same time. Helena, though she appeared to be looking the other way, immediately said, 'Oh, do smoke, anyone', and so we drew out our pipes. Thus bidden, Mark finished what he was playing on the piano and came over to the fire with his own pipe to join us.

'You seem happier today than when I last saw you, Mark', said Dickie in his blunt way.

'Ah, well, it seems that I'm no longer everyone's favourite suspect. What the Guards might be thinking is anyone's guess, but at least I can go about my business now without encountering black looks from perfect strangers. I seem to be *passé*. At any rate, the betting has shifted to a new runner.'

'Really?' said Dickie. 'I seem to be out of the loop for suspect-gossip. Who are they pitching on now?'

THE SERPENT IN THE GARDEN

'The feeling seems to be that Steve Blackmore has had rather too many winners of late to be altogether above board; and we all know that Michael took rather a keen interest in that sort of thing.'

At this I felt as if someone had delivered a blow between my shoulder blades. Stephen Blackmore! Stevie had been one of my earliest friends, a great rival and pal in Pony Club days, and hunting companion afterwards. The black injustice of this was even worse than fixing on Mark had been. Mark at least was unmarried, and not local. He was only among us for a year, to catalogue the furnishings of the Abbey. But Steve was not only Ardliss born and bred, he was a widower bringing up two children on his own. And his profession made any malicious gossip particularly dangerous.

'But this is outrageous!' I spluttered, having inhaled sharply on hearing the news. 'That sort of rumour is very dangerous to a trainer. If it got back to the Jockey Club it could cause any amount of mischief.'

'Oh, everyone in racing is the perpetual subject of rumours', Dickie said. 'The great problem for the Jockey Club is sifting through them all. I can't see them worrying about what people here are saying, unless the Guards come up with some evidence.'

'But all the same', I objected, 'it's a dreadfully malicious thing to speculate about.'

'Oh I grant you that,' said Dickie; 'but if anyone gets too enthusiastic in their gossip it will give Steve the chance to sue them for slander; which is the sort of thing he would probably enjoy.'

There was little I could say in reply to this. It was true that Steve rather relished a fight. Those who didn't know him well regarded him as taciturn, and someone who would bear a grudge for a long time, for grievances real or imagined. With his rugged looks and fiery black eyes, his appearance lent itself to this image. Only his family and old friends knew how kind and patient he could be to those he trusted.

Our conversation had obviously been overheard by the others in the room. From her sofa I heard Maria's mellifluous, softly accented voice indignantly exclaim, 'It is terrible, what people will say, and the damage it can do. We should not make accusations when we don't even know what has happened. The police don't even seem to know.'

'Indeed', Helena said. 'It is indefensible to suspect, let alone accuse, anyone until we are given some reason by the police to do so. It is particularly important that those of us who live together here should maintain a charitable disposition, both to one another and to everyone else. We must never lose sight of the fact that this is a temporary state of affairs. Once Michael's killer is arrested and convicted, we will all have to continue living with each other.'

Unfortunately Helena's attempt to bring her sensible advice to bear only begged the question: Which of us would be left living here after the arrest? What if the murderer was indeed among us?

4
Blandings

The notable attraction at Blandings, which draws most of the tourists who come to see the gardens, is a series of inter-linking pools formed from what was originally a small, lazy stream. Each of these pools constitutes a micro-habitat for some of the specimens that William Chancellor brings back from his travels. The immediate response most people have to this practice is, of course, fear of the consequences of introducing alien flora and fauna into a new environment. But there is no one more keenly aware than William of that sort of danger; he is indeed at the forefront of efforts to halt the advance of the grey squirrel through Ireland. So the ponds do not pose that sort of threat. Some of the species require such a refined environment that they would perish were they to venture beyond their specially prepared area. Others have been subjected to some sort of process, possibly irradiation, which effects little entomological vasectomies and hysterectomies, as it were, upon them, rendering the newcomers harmless if they stray.

You will gather from these comments that I have not made an extensive study of zoology, or indeed of biology of any sort. And I would like to clarify at the outset that my knowledge even of geography is poor. If it had been left to me, these sciences would have remained at about Herodotus' or Cosmas Indicopleustes' level of

development. And if you reported to me that you had just
been to the zoo to see the rocs and the hippodragons, I
should be inclined to believe you. So please refrain from
writing to me with information about my scientific
inaccuracies. My response will resemble that of Sherlock
Holmes when Dr. Watson discovered that he (Holmes)
did not know that the earth revolved around the sun.
Having been informed of such facts I will immediately
make every effort to forget them, since they would
otherwise occupy space in my brain more usefully
dedicated to other things. Any correspondence of this
type that I receive will therefore be shredded
immediately and dedicated to the comfort of
Theophrastes.

On the afternoon following the police raid (as we
liked to call it among ourselves) I was walking down the
pond path, seeking to soothe my jangled nerves and also
trying to order my mind, to make what sense I could of
events. Approaching the Himalayan peacock-dragonfly
pond I came upon Helena making her rounds, and
possibly putting out dragonfly food. She was well-
wrapped in a waterproof jacket, tweed skirt and
gumboots, and accompanied by her tortoiseshell cat,
Cleopatra. Cleopatra is the acknowledged diva among
the Abbey cats, and therefore not best friends with
Theophrastes I'm afraid. The two of them circled each
other with contemptuous disdain. 'Oh Robbie, hello' said
Helena. 'Have you seen the babies that have just
hatched?'

THE SERPENT IN THE GARDEN

I duly admired the iridescent infants. 'Well, the dragonflies have certainly settled in,' I observed, watching them flit in and out of a small Buddhist temple in the midst of their pond, and hover about the lily pads. 'I believe you have had some trouble with the Mesopotamian spotted newts' I said, always glad of an opportunity to show an interest in the pond inhabitants.

'Yes, but we've got that sorted out finally. We've got the insects segregated, and the various sorts of newts in their pools, and the Appalachian swamp frogs in theirs – they have a little log cabin, have you seen it? And some hickory and American dogwood. I've just come up from the new pond that will have the Tibetan Golden Salamanders and the Okinawan Sampan Butterflies, and I'm hoping they don't upset the balance again. William will bring these things home and only then start worrying about where to put them. I have hardly any space on my kitchen window-sill for all the spawn and larvae.'

'It must be helpful to have Dr. Crespi staying with you', I said.

'Yes, well, it is when I can get hold of her. Would you believe that her specialism is Irish newts? She is here to make a survey of their population numbers and distribution. We obviously have indigenous newts and frogs catered for around the place, but why does a Roman herpetologist end up falling in love with Irish newts? So many people seem doomed to become fascinated with things they can't find in their own country. Look at poor little Mr Moto with his Norman towers and megalithic tombs. There must be any number of equally interesting things in the Orient, but his heart has always yearned after druids and knights.'

'Well,' I suggested, 'at least you have the advantage that the world tends to come to you, both in the form of humans, and also as your animal and vegetable guests.'

'Well, yes, I suppose one must look on the bright side,' said Helena doubtfully; 'but they keep me very tied at home, especially since William is perpetually abroad seeking out this and that and bringing it home in a jar. His name is spoken among agricultural import officers with a fearful hush. And now, just as things are settling nicely for a bit I've had sniffer dogs terrifying all the amphibians. They've taken away the quad bike, by the way, which has incensed everyone on the farm. Billy has been working to rule pending a replacement. And on top of everything, I've been trying to hold out against the Guards, who have been agitating to be allowed to dredge the ponds! Can you imagine! I told them that they would have to approach William personally if they wanted to touch the ponds, and that if they did I would take myself off under an alias to some warm, sunny spot until the dust settled. It's such a relief it didn't come to that. But what a pity about poor Debbie, isn't it? It must have been such a shock for her.'

Now this I didn't follow. 'Debbie English in the Stables? Why, what's happened?'

'Oh, I thought perhaps you had heard; people seem to hear everything somehow, almost before it's happened. Debbie appears to have found the whatever it was they used to killed Michael with, tangled up in some of those wire thingies she makes.'

I was stunned. Debbie inhabited a renovated stable block immediately opposite the Slatterys. At least, that isn't strictly speaking the case; she was married and lived in a village nearby. But she rented the stable block as her workshop, which was the nearest building to Michael's house. It was hard to credit there being anything left for Debbie to find if the Guards had run their fine-toothed comb over the workshop. I confess to experiencing a certain smugness at the thought of them running around the Abbey courtyard in circles, before they had made an exhaustive check of the area surrounding Michael's house.

In any case, I'm afraid that murder weapons rouse my curiosity as much as they do anyone's, so taking my leave of Helena I hurried back to the Abbey and collected my scooter, Theophrastes jumping into his basket at the front. It was a mere matter of minutes to leave the outer courtyard and make my way down the road and out the back gate of the park, and then turn left and down to Debbie's workshop. I parked my scooter outside her gate, since the stable yard, although now unoccupied by horses, has a tendency to be muddy. Theophrastes picked his way with care, ears twitching suspiciously. Looking over at the Slatterys' house I noticed that everyone seemed to be out. It then occurred to me that there was indeed no one about at all; Billy and Max were of course busy with their evening work, so the pair of semi-detached houses they occupied were also empty. I fell to musing how easy it might have been for someone to murder Michael here unobserved, and then take any amount of time deciding how and where to dispose of the body. There was a spattering of rain as clouds began to cover the weak autumn sun. I shivered involuntarily. I began to fancy that there was something uncanny in the absolute silence of the place, and I felt an unaccountable urge to retrieve my scooter and leave. But I shook myself to dispel such foolishness, and entered the stable yard. The mood refused to leave me, however, and the complete silence, and total absence, it appeared, of any living thing, made me approach the stable block slowly, and with a soft tread. For some reason, I felt unwilling to go directly to the door and knock or call out, so I decided to look in at the window first. Even this made me uneasy however, so approaching the window from the side, I cautiously peered in, and was met by a contorted face, frozen in a silent scream. I fell back against the wall, my heart racing.

Now some people care for that sort of thing, but I have to confess that I regard it as a pity that an academically trained sculptress should devote so much of her time to depicting states of neurosis — or in the case of this particular figure, I should say psychosis. Debbie did very beautiful charcoal drawings, and made classically composed portrait busts to commission, but left to her own creative devices she went in for these agonised bodies. I realise that tastes vary, and that artists have to express their own unique vision; but just at that moment I would happily have dispensed with this particular manifestation of *angst*. My heart was pounding and my palms clammy as I knocked and went in.

The inside of a sculptor's studio is a confusing labyrinth. Apart from finished and partially-finished pieces, there are studies in clay, and casts; walls are covered with drawings, photographs, measured diagrams, and plans for finished pieces. There are drawing boards, basins of water and strips of linen, and work tables covered in things. And everywhere amongst it all are bits of metal wire and bolts and joints, in various states of assembly: these are the 'wire thingies' referred to by Helena, armatures which serve as the skeletal framework around which clay figures can be modelled, and which keep them from collapsing. It seems that someone had entered Debbie's studio and attached the spanner that killed Michael to a semi-constructed armature that was in preparation for a full-life figure. Apart from being rather larger than a usual piece of armature it was not very conspicuous, being tucked away in a dark corner. So it was only when Debbie began rummaging through her bits and pieces with the intention of finishing it that she found the incongruous spanner where it had been attached. She had great presence of mind; realising immediately what it must be, she refrained from handling it and rang Helena, who informed the Guards, who had come and taken it away — happily having despaired of finding any further evidence in the jumble of the studio, which had in any case been in use continuously since the murder.

I was unsure at first whether there was anyone at home. 'Hello', I called out cautiously.

'Hello?' came Debbie's cheerful reply. Her slim form emerged from the shadows as she removed clay-covered rubber gloves and came towards me. 'Oh, hello Robbie. If you've come to examine exhibit A, you're too late; they've taken it away in a plastic bag. It looked pretty clean to me, but there you are.'

'You're awfully calm and serene, given the circumstances. Doesn't it make you jittery, being in here alone with no one about?'

'Well, actually you've just missed the rush. There have been Guards by the score, for one thing. They seem to have found the murder scene, behind the Slatterys' house. They've put up a little tent over it, and there is actually someone there guarding it, though you can't see him from here. That's why there's no one at home there. Helena came and spoke to Sinead, who has taken the boys to their grandmother for a few days. Then, after the Guards moved off, lots of curious people came to see what was going on. I began to think I ought to sell tickets for admission! If anything, the sight-seers put me off my stride even more than the Guards had. I haven't been able to get anything done as a result, so I thought I would clean up a bit in the meantime.'

I reflected with embarrassment that I was but another such sight-seer. Debbie must have noticed my expression, because she laughed and said, 'So you see I'm not doing anything now that can't bear interruption. Would you like a cup of tea?' And so, though I felt rather ashamed to take up yet more of her lost working day, we had tea and she showed me the famous armature, and just where the spanner had been attached. We then proceeded to talk about her work, her commissions and her teaching. It occurred to me how much I missed this sort of normal conversation, so used had I become already to an ever-present atmosphere of gossip and speculation. Little did I know then how much longer we would be living in that atmosphere, and how much more intense it was to become! 'You know, my dear', I said at length, 'I must really thank you for our chat. It is so refreshing to talk about other things than the murder. You are very wise to be able to keep your perspective so well.'

Debbie thought a moment and then smiled. 'Actually, it takes a lot to get an artist to think of anything other than work! In any case, if the murder really took place next door, and the murderer hid the weapon here, this is the last place he would want to return to. I dare say this will be the end of any excitement up here.'

While applauding Debbie's good sense, I couldn't help but feel that this was a premature confidence. It did not seem to have occurred to her that the murder weapon could have been placed in her studio at any time since the murder. Indeed, that might well explain why the Guards had not found it during their first search. The murderer might well have been watching Debbie, waiting for her to leave the coast clear. Any further extrapolation of the murder having taken place in this remote part of the estate, inhabited by only four adults, a few small boys and a score of spaniels, didn't bear thinking about. But not wishing to say anything to cause her unease, I simply thanked Debbie again for tea, and made my farewell. Retrieving my scooter I looked once again at the empty house opposite, and imagined the murder scene behind it, and its silent guardian. How curious, I thought, that someone with so much artistic instinct as Debbie, should apparently be so unsusceptible to atmosphere. There seemed to me to be a hollow and chill feeling to the place. Even the black silage bags in the field beside the Slatterys' house took on a sinister aspect, their white smiley faces (the distinctive mark of Blandings silage bags) seeming to leer at me ghoulishly in the twilight.

It will therefore doubtless sound odd when I say that, turning my scooter in preparation to leave, it was with a warmth of welcome that I heard the steady trot of horses approaching from the gloom of the forest path behind me. How it was I cannot say, but I knew those horses before I saw them. I set aside my scooter once more, and walked back towards the emerging shadows, until I could make out the form of Steve Blackmore, wearing the ill-humoured scowl that had become habitual since his wife's tragic death two years before. But as he saw me the lines left his face and his old familiar smile appeared. 'Hello stranger!' he said, as his two girls came into focus behind him.

'Hello Lucy, Alice', I said as they reached me. 'Just hacking out?'

THE SERPENT IN THE GARDEN

'We've been down to the galloping green', said young Alice happily.

'I thought you were training eventers now Lucy', I ventured. Lucy was 25, an AI, and had recently found a good job at a riding school *cum* eventers' yard.

'Yeah, well, I came home for a day off' she said, giving her father a sideways look.

'And Dad's got you working, is that it?'

We all laughed. I wondered whether Steve had heard the rumours about him, and if he hadn't, whether that was for the best; or whether I ought to find an occasion for telling him. I knew that I was one of the few people who could speak to him about such a thing without him taking offense.

'Sapphire's looking very fit, Steve', I said, scratching her nose.

'We miss you at the yard, Robbie', he said kindly. 'When are you going to come out with us again? We'll give you whoever you like. It's undignified going about on that piddly little thing' — this with a sharp look towards my scooter.

I was moved. How unlike Steve's misanthropic image this was. He was, as I have said, a warm friend to those whom he trusted. 'I'll be back just as soon as the chiropractor finishes sorting my shoulder out, believe me', I said. 'As for the scooter, it fits into my parking slot, which is more than I could say for one of Sapphire's chums!'

'Did you hear that people think Daddy did the murder', Alice piped up with a grin. Lucy gave her a scowl, and I glanced at Steve. But to my relief he started laughing, an incongruous sound in that dreary setting. 'As if I could stand to speak to that unctuous little worm, let alone do business with him.' Lucy stirred uneasily in her saddle, looking unhappily at the ground. Catching my expression, though, Steve smiled again and said gently, 'Now, don't you worry about me, Robbie. The woods are thick with people who had a much better reason to have killed him than I ever did. The most I was ever tempted to do was to kick his backside for being so slimy. It must be a mercy for his family to be rid of him.'

'Dad!' said Lucy, looking alarmed.

Despite the fact that I knew Sinead to be away, I couldn't help casting a nervous glance at the house. It must be said that by this point the cheerfulness of our meeting was waning, and I was suddenly aware of how dark and chill the evening was becoming. It was getting past time for them all to be back home. Aware that I could hardly accompany them on my scooter and still converse, I waved them farewell and went on my way, my mind racing more feverishly than ever.

5
Dinner with Fr Enda

Faithful to his word in this (as doubtless in all things), it was not long after Michael's funeral that Fr. Enda assembled a clerical pow-wow over his dining table. As well as the Carringtons, there were Fr. Tom from Drum, Fr. Reg (Enda's curate), and Fr. Chris, an elderly predecessor of Enda's, renowned for his unexpectedly witty and irreverent contributions to social gatherings. Fr. Chris was indeed so full of spirit that Matthew Carrington had once threatened to turn up the settings on his motorised zimmer frame and take him on for a race.

Of all the hospitable tables and sitting rooms in their parish (and they are many), it must be said that Fr. Enda's dinner parties were regarded by Angela as especial treats, and reminded her most of her Italian home. As well as the opulence of his table, with regards to both food and drink (I shall not embark upon the glories of his cellar), Fr. Enda is a great *connoisseur* of art, and his house is adorned with many icons and works of western religious art, both originals and copies of the highest quality. It was therefore not long after the party had moved from the comfort of Enda's sitting room, relinquishing its roaring fire and rare sherry, to take their places in the dining room, that their cares had faded, and the conversation grew increasingly relaxed and jocular.

'I didn't envy you the funeral, Enda, with all that media attention and the ambiguity of the circumstances,' Matthew Carrington said during a pause after sorbet.

'Nor I;' said Fr Tom, smiling at Enda. 'I was glad to be on holiday and leave it to you!'

'I'll return the favour one day,' replied Enda.

'There can't have been many deaths in the parish as sensational as that one,' continued Matthew. There was a low demurring noise from the other clergy.

'Oh, we've had some hair-raisers, haven't we?' Enda asked, as Tom, Reg and Chris assented. 'Not so much media attention perhaps, but just as tricky in other ways. And this isn't the first death surrounded by rumour, not by a long mark.'

'Nor the first dramatic one. We've had some dreadful accidents over the years,' said Tom, casting rather a pall over the subject.

'Not the first sensational one either,' said Chris: 'I remember one of your predecessors, Matthew. You won't have known him. Trevor Haddock. Had a way of rubbing people up the wrong way.' At this the others burst out laughing. 'So when he died his funeral was here in Ardliss, but he had his body cremated. Then, he had left instructions for a fireworks display to be put on for the town, here in the Square. What he didn't tell people was that he had arranged to have his ashes sent up with the fireworks, where they exploded over everyone, and ended up as grit in their eyes. He no doubt enjoyed the sight from wherever he was looking on.'

53

'Ah,' said Matthew, as the others guffawed at the memory. 'It seems my parishioners have been rather circumspect in what they have told me about my predecessors.'

'Oh, well, I suppose they were a mixed bag, like in most parishes,' Enda said. 'I'd say that the real problems arise from these very long interregna like the one before you. It takes the heart out of a parish to go for too long without their own clergy. Mind you, the people who looked after your parish during that time, certainly down at this end, were very good and conscientious. But most of them are still in the diocese, so you'll know that better than I do.'

'It was interesting for us all when Barbara came for six months. I don't think most of us had encountered any women clergy first hand before, even in your parish. I must say that she became very popular, though,' said Tom as the other assented.

'Yes indeed,' said Enda. 'I think the Church of Ireland people were a bit disconcerted at first, but by the time Barbara left to go back to Canada there was a real sadness.'

'I wonder if it will ever catch on in the Catholic Church,' said Chris mischievously. 'We have a lot of religious sisters who would make marvelous priests.'

Enda, Tom and Reg emitted groans, while Matthew chuckled.

'Oh, please don't start;' said Tom. 'We've heard it all so many times, the arguments for and against. And it only ends up going round in circles.'

J.E. RUTHERFORD

'It's generally taken to be a question of authority and tradition,' Matthew said, 'but surely it is really a matter of anthropology. What is it to be human, and are we really suggesting that female humanity differs from male humanity? And if so, in what way? Do we believe that males participate in a fuller humanity than females? One of the great strengths of the Fathers, certainly from Athanasius onwards, was their awareness of the inextricable connection between anthropology and soteriology. Of course, for them the pressing need was to safeguard the role of Christ's humanity in our salvation.' The others murmured their agreement.

' "What is not assumed is not saved",' said Chris.

'Exactly,' continued Matthew. 'What started off for the Fathers as the need to affirm that Christ was completely human, so that he could be said to have saved humanity completely, has turned up again for us now, the other way round: We are now having to affirm the complete humanity of both sexes in order to believe that Christ saves them both equally. If "what is not assumed is not saved", then Christ assumed the same humanity as females, as well as males. So far, everyone agrees. But to have women preside at the Eucharist confronts us with a problem most of us don't acknowledge that we have. We accept that a male priest, in representing Christ in the celebration, represents female as well as male humanity. But we rebel against the implicit affirmation that a woman priest can represent male as well as female humanity. I think that we all still have an innate, unacknowledged belief that women are not completely human, in the way that men are. Men can represent them, but they can't represent men. For me, women priests are a way of safeguarding Christian anthropology.'

Having been accustomed to this sort of conversation from early youth, Angela found her attention drifting from this absorbing subject. Her eyes settled, as they so often did at Enda's parties, on the lovely paintings in his dining room. When Enda rose to offer dessert wines Angela took the opportunity to walk over to a *Caravaggesque* historical portrait that she had always found intriguing. She wished that she could examine it in daylight. Handing her a glass of Marsala, Enda joined her.

'It really is uncommonly good,' Angela said. 'If you saw it on its own somewhere, say in a grand *palazzo*, you would assume it was genuine. Is it a copy, or an imitation of his style? I don't remember seeing the *motif* before.'

'Well,' said Enda, pleased to have his collection admired by an artist, 'to be honest with you I don't know. I'm a great admirer of Caravaggio, and when I saw this I felt I really had to have it. But I'm not an expert on all his work, so I couldn't say whether there's an original of this somewhere.'

'And of course, there are more originals coming to light all the time,' observed Angela. 'Did you read about the one that had been languishing in the royal collection in London for a couple of hundred years, leaning against a wall? It has only just now been attributed to Caravaggio.' Still gazing at the painting, she continued, 'Now this, I feel sure, was painted by an Italian copyist. Not in Florence; it would be more self-conscious if it had been. And not in *Napoli*; it would be cruder. I should say that this artist works in either Rome or Milan.'

'Oh, yes, I get all my reproductions in Rome;' said Enda with animation. 'I have a friend there who brought me to see the work of this particular fellow — his name's on the back somewhere. Rome is filled with reproductions of the masters, as you will know yourself. But this fellow seemed particularly good.'

'He is indeed,' said Angela, turning to Enda and smiling. 'Most of the copies you find in Italy are no better than elaborate souvenirs; pretty things to take home, but without the depth and subtlety of the originals. The *Rinascimento* resulted in schools of convention, and their techniques are quite easy to copy. The leaders among artists always have their own particular techniques, and palettes, in addition, and these too lend themselves to imitation. But the geniuses, like Caravaggio, confront us with the paradoxes of the human psyche with a shock that is almost physical; and they generally do it with such technical economy that we feel, as the Greeks used to, that such artists work under the inspiration of the gods. Caravaggio could convey more with one thin, chalk-like brush stroke on a black ground than most artists could convey with all the paint and all the time in the world at their disposal. That's what intrigues me about this painting. Caravaggio's palette is easy enough for a good artist to copy. But the economy and sureness of the brush work that seems to be here — I can't see it very well — speak of a really great talent. I particularly admire the character he has got in St Peter's face. And the feet are very bold, very confident. They are what make me think that this is an imitation rather than a copy. I can't imagine Caravaggio taking another chance with dirty feet after his trouble over the pilgrims.'

'No,' said Enda, 'though this might have been painted before that, or for a patron who cared more for earthy humanity. Or of course, he might have done it just to be contrary, which is not hard to imagine.'

'True,' said Angela. 'There is never any certainty in trying to reconstruct the circumstances of the creation of any work of art, especially without any contemporary written account. If you don't mind,' she said, 'I would love to know who painted this. Perhaps I could come round some day and make a note of his name, and the address of his studio.'

'Of course,' said Enda, delighted. 'His things are quite a bit more expensive than the average copy, but I'm glad you agree that he's worth it.'

Angela longed to know exactly how much a painting like this sold for, straight from the artist's studio. She hoped it was enough to keep the artist on the straight and narrow, rather than dabbling in less reputable but more lucrative forms of copying.

'I hope that he paints his own things, too; it would be awful if he just copies masters,' she thought to herself. But Angela knew better than most that the inexorable law of the market is such that it is the name of the artist that sells the painting, not the beauty and quality of the work.

As they gradually took up their glasses to move back to the sitting room for coffee, the conversation inevitably took a gastronomic turn.

'A beautiful dinner, as usual, Enda,' said Chris as he was helped into a chair by the fire. 'The scallops were absolutely succulent. Where did you find them?'

'I'll bet that they came from *Fishy Business*, didn't they? I get all my fish from them, and I know that Helena does too,' said Angela.

'Ah, there aren't any secrets in Ardliss. I do use *Fishy Business*. They are so reliable. I had their salmon fillets for the Apostolic Nuncio when he was here. Wonderful,' said Enda.

'And the partridges!' exclaimed Tom, at which everyone emitted a communal 'Ahh!'

'That was so clever, you know, to split them in half before roasting them gently. It takes great courage, that, because the basting is essential to prevent them drying out. I must admit that I generally take the safe way out and braise them,' said Angela.

'Now I've never tried that,' said Enda. 'You must give me the recipe. Though I'm not often given partridges.'

'It works as well with quails, and even pheasants,' said Angela.

'Oh, stop! I'm too full to talk about food,' said Reg.

THE SERPENT IN THE GARDEN

'Let's talk about wine, then!' said Chris, holding his glass of ruby port to the light of the fire.

'Yes, let's do!' said Matthew. 'We can start by quizzing Enda about his wine importer. I sometimes suspect you of being the wine correspondent for *La Compressa*, Enda. You can't possibly bring all your stock back with you from your trips to the Continent.'

'No, indeed. As a matter of fact I have almost everything sent to me directly through local dealers in France, Spain, Italy and Portugal. It's taken a bit of time building up the connections, but it's been worth it. Interestingly, the fellow I go through in Italy is the same friend who introduced me to the artist we were talking about, Angela. It was just luck that I found out how good a supplier he is, because it wouldn't have occurred to me to investigate Rome as a source. I had been nosing around Piedmont and Tuscany, but of course the world had gone ahead of me. The price of wine in Italy is outrageous unless you get off the beaten track; and there's not much of that left. So he's been a closely guarded secret — not that I would object to adding anything any of you might want to my own orders,' he added gallantly.

'In fact, I've been able to relax a bit since Michael died,' he continued after a pause. 'It might sound uncharitable of me, but I really got annoyed at the way he wanted to ferret out my wine suppliers. I even caught him examining my shipments once. Of course, there was no harm in it really, but it irritated me that he seemed to want to poach my contacts, when it has taken me so long to build them up. I'm afraid that I took rather a delight in frustrating him. I felt sure that he would have tried to use them to set up a direct wine import business himself, probably using all my favourite labels.'

'Of course he would have,' said Chris. 'That would have been just the like of him. Remember the little disused convent he bought from the parish for a song? Years ago, it was. He stripped out all the woodwork and ornaments and sold them abroad for twice what he had paid for the whole building, and then left the rest a derelict ruin. You can see it still, out along the Dublin Road, Matthew, if you've the heart to look.'

'Yes, I'm afraid that Michael wasn't a very nice fellow to deal with,' said Enda.

'Well, at least he wasn't your parishioner, even if you did have to bury him!' said Tom with feeling, Blandings falling as it does within the parish of Drum. 'And so devout. He never missed Mass, or Confession. It was depressing to see how little improvement it made in his character.'

'Ah,' said Chris. 'But remember what Evelyn Waugh said when he was asked how he, as a Catholic, could be so rude? He said, "Just imagine what I would be like if I *wasn't* a Catholic"!'

'Good Lord,' said Enda as everyone laughed. 'Do you mean to say that Michael might have been even worse?'

'Well, we would have thought a lot worse of him if that golf course scheme had gone ahead', said Matthew.

61

There was an abrupt silence. Then '*What?*' erupted from all sides. Matthew looked about in surprise.

'Oh, I'm sorry; I thought everyone knew. I'm usually the last one in on the gossip. Apparently Michael was a silent partner with Dickie Bird on the development plans for the big field on the Drum Road — beside our school, you know.'

'But that has planning permission for housing, surely.' said Enda.

'Yes, and that's what Dickie has really wanted to go for, it seems. I dare say that he will now, because Sinead was saying to me, when I saw her today, that she agrees with Dickie. But Michael had thought that there would be more to be made out of a driving range and putting course. He wanted to build a state of the art club house to attract people from all three counties, and maybe even further afield. You know what people will pay for a first rate facility of that sort.'

'But where would they park?' asked Reg.

'Yes, that's what I wondered, too', said Matthew. 'It's a big piece of land, but I don't see how you could have a driving range, putting course, and club house, and still have enough parking space for the crowds who would want to come. And building an underground car park wouldn't really be feasible. In a way, it would have been a good idea if it hadn't been so ambitious. The land really isn't suited to building, as I suspect will become apparent. Using it for sport was actually a good idea. But there you have Michael all over, not content with a modest plan. Mind you, an extra three hundred houses in the town isn't a modest plan, either.'

'Is it three hundred?' gasped Enda. 'I thought it was only about a hundred.'

'Oh, no, Sinead has shown me the plans. Though I should have said three hundred *dwellings*. There are to be flats and apartments as well as semi-detached and detached houses. And each dwelling has to have two car spaces, which could give us six hundred extra cars in town, all emerging to work and school in the morning, and returning in the evening.'

'But that's appalling!' said Tom. 'Surely there ought to be some sort of protest!'

'I suppose we could get on to the environment people,' said Chris.

'Or maybe the heritage people,' said Angela.

'Well, I must admit that I was rather alarmed myself when it was all explained to me, but I really didn't know what to say,' said Matthew.

'Of course not,' said Enda. 'Under the circumstances, no one would want to have any sort of unpleasantness with Sinead. But as for Dickie Bird, I think he would be advised to keep a low profile, under the circumstances.'

By this time everyone was wider awake than ought to have been the case, given the fire, food and wine. What with golf courses, housing developments, and who knows what else to anticipate, it seemed that Michael's legacy was still very much alive, however dead he himself might be. As the party rose to say goodnight, and wrap themselves against the cold and dark, Angela wondered uneasily where it would all lead, and whether Michael's death was the beginning rather than the end of the drama.

J.E. RUTHERFORD

6
The Physiotherapist's Tale

Reversing her car out of its parking space and easing it through the courtyard gate, Cathy was vividly aware of the twinges in her knee. The growing chill of early December was making it clear to her that sooner or later, with inexorable inevitability, it would need to be replaced. She had been on a waiting list for some time, but had hoped that the minor surgery she had had in the summer might sort things out sufficiently to be going on with. But there was no point in deceiving herself into believing that the knee was going to improve substantially on what it was like at the moment. Nevertheless, in the meantime it was important to keep her physiotherapy appointments; and so, driving slowly up from the Abbey to the main road through the park, she turned right and down the long avenue of beech and oak, and out the main gate to the Ardliss road. After checking carefully (for the traffic that comes round the bend by the gate tends to hurtle past at a terrifying speed), she turned left and made her way to the clinic that we are fortunate to have in the nearby village of Drum.

Like most rural Church of Ireland parishes, ours covers a large geographical area; as I have already explained, it incorporates substantial portions of two counties and a sliver of a third. The western boundary of the parish, and indeed of our diocese, follows the contours of high ground, which then drops steeply into lower, boggy land. From Drum it is possible on a clear day to gaze in a wide arc from North to West to South without seeing any end to the low ground, only the twinkle of Lough Coile to the north, and beyond it the elusive promise of distant mountains. The parish extends for a bit onto the bog, but eventually habitations become more scarce; and the neighbouring parish to the west seems a world away. It was on such a bright, clear day as this that Cathy set out for the clinic. When the weather was good, she liked to make a detour to the edge of the bog for the view, before going to her appointment. Afterwards would hardly be possible, since she always felt that her leg had been put through a mangle by the time her physiotherapy session was over. It must also be confessed that she had a certain dread of these appointments, and tended to put them off as long as possible. She was certain that every neglected stretch and exercise of the previous week would be apparent to the practitioner at first sight, and like most patients in similar circumstances she was guiltily aware that there had been a fair degree of such neglect recently. Doing the exercises had come to seem like a form of masochism, and she was not that way inclined.

At last, however, there was no excuse for delaying the inevitable any longer. She returned to the clinic and steeled herself for the ordeal to come. Now to meet Judy, the physiotherapist, after the preceding narrative, one would be surprised to think that she could be capable of inspiring such dread. Small and cheerful, with an engaging American accent, Judy was indeed a pleasant person to encounter. But all round her office were rather intimidating intimations of her profession. For Judy, as has been mentioned already, was greatly given to utilising the latest devices and machines available for the manipulation of muscles and joints. It was from Judy that Matthew Carrington had learnt of the neck-stretching machine, which had so impressed him that he bought one of his own. Cathy, it must be said, had not encountered any therapeutic device in Judy's arsenal that held the least allure for her. After the initial greetings, Cathy sat down before Judy, unrolled the appropriate stocking, and awaited the verdict.

'Not too bad, really,' said Judy, expertly probing the joint with the sure instinct of an Inquisitor. Cathy closed her eyes to the pain, but had to admit to herself that it was not very much greater than what had now become her habitual discomfort. 'Have you been doing your exercises?' Judy continued.

'Well, on and off, I'm afraid,' Cathy replied honestly. 'I'm always a little worried that I'm not doing them properly, and that I'm going to do more harm than good if I persist.'

'I know,' said Judy, leading Cathy over to the couch and assisting her to get up. 'But really, you know, the more you skip your exercises, the stiffer the knee will get, and the more it will hurt when you try to move it. It really is a vicious circle. Now, let's get you on the traction machine for a minute, and try some flexion. First I'm going to apply a little ice, though, to help get some of that inflammation down.' After patting the knee joint carefully with ice packs, Judy drew down from the ceiling what looked to Cathy like a noose, and gently attached it to the appropriate leg. 'Now, we'll just do some straightening exercises,' she said, retracting the attachment back towards the ceiling, causing Cathy to sympathise with all those who had ever endured being stretched on racks. 'Stretch, flex; stretch, flex;' said Judy, slowly tightening and loosening the device. Gradually, Cathy had to admit, the joint did begin to move more freely. It also acquired a numb sensation, which Cathy could only regard with relief. 'Now, lets try some deep flexes,' Judy continued, unhooking the machine. 'How far can you bend your knee?' she asked.

'Not enough to kneel right down,' replied Cathy. So Judy worked on folding the knee as far back as was possible, back and forth for several rounds.

'Have you tried acupuncture for the pain and inflammation?' she asked, as Cathy was beginning to believe that she was being prepared for shrink-wrapping.

'Oh, you know, I've tried that, but it's all temporary anyhow, and by the time I've driven there and back I'm exhausted. I'm just resigned now to waiting for the replacement.'

'Yes, I'm afraid that's all that can really be done now. We talked about the x-rays last time. There's nothing I can really do except keep you as mobile as possible in the meantime, especially so you can drive.'

'Oh, yes, I appreciate that,' said Cathy, as Judy gently laid her leg straight again on the couch. 'I really would be in a pickle if I couldn't drive. But what I really miss most is not being able to do my own gardening. It is so frustrating having to stand over a border and try to explain to someone else what you want done. You want to get your own hands on it; what you would do yourself isn't something you can explain to someone else. But if I try to kneel down and get at things, I can hardly straighten my leg again afterwards, and it feels dreadful for days.'

'You really shouldn't do that,' said Judy seriously, stopping to look Cathy in the eyes. 'Really. The joint is too deteriorated, and you could end up completely crippled, and in a great deal of pain. Now to finish today I'm going to put you on the TENS machine for a few minutes, to soothe the inflammation and promote healing in the surrounding tissue.' Drawing forward a table with a black box on it, Judy took its attached wires and, connecting them to pads, placed them at various points on Cathy's knee. She then sat opposite Cathy as the tiny prickling pulses began to work. 'Tell me if it's too much,' she said. 'No, that's about right,' said Cathy. They sat in silence for a few minutes, until, gazing round the room, Cathy caught sight of some brochures advertising cruises in the South China Sea.

'Are you going on holiday?' she asked conversationally.

Following her glance, Judy's eyes shone and she said, 'Not exactly. Max and I are planning our honeymoon.'

'Max from the Abbey farm? Oh, my dear, my very best wishes. Have you just recently got engaged?'

'Well, no, actually,' continued Judy happily. 'We've been engaged for over a year, but we've been trying to raise the money to make it possible for me only to work part-time. There's no point in getting married at all if I'm working nine to five every day, and he's working all hours. We wouldn't see any more of each other than we do now.'

'No, quite. But, you'll excuse me, I hope; it's just that I would have thought that Max's income would be more than sufficient to marry on. He's a qualified farm manager, after all, and I know that the house is small, but —'

At this point, Judy became uneasy, and her eyes dropped. 'No, of course; everything you say is true. But; I shouldn't talk about this to anyone, but I know you won't say . . .'

'Oh, I am so sorry,' said Cathy quickly, mortified; 'I really didn't mean to pry.'

'No, no; I'd like to tell someone, because I don't have anyone to talk to about it, and it's not something I would want to happen again.'

'Well, of course I'll keep any confidence you care to share with me . . .'

Judy paused, and for a while Cathy assumed that she had thought better of continuing. But then, 'It was those card parties,' she blurted out. 'That's what worried me right from the start. It's all over now because that horrible man is dead, but it was really scary at the time.

First it was just a friendly game of cards after work, but then more people started to play, and of course it was always for money. I had never thought that Max was like that. He works so hard, and he always pays for everything up front; he won't even use his credit card except for emergencies. And so I thought that we didn't have any problems. But then he kept putting the wedding off, and I thought he had cold feet. So I confronted him about it, and at last he admitted that he owed thousands of euros to the other players. It was going to take years to pay back. I was really upset, because I never thought Max was the sort of guy to get an addiction. But on the other hand, once I thought about it, I could see that in a way his work is like an addiction. He doesn't give up until he succeeds at something, and the more in debt he got, the more he played to get out of it. I didn't know what to do. And there was no one I could talk to without getting Max into trouble.'

'Do you mean to say,' said Cathy, trembling with indignation and sitting upright despite the wires, 'that Michael Slattery was organising poker games?'

'Well,' said Judy, near to tears with the relief of finally being able to unburden herself, 'I just know that he introduced Max to the other players. I don't know that he played himself. Probably not; *he* wouldn't have done anything risky. But after he was killed, the other players all got scared, and they had a meeting and told Max to say that the games had never taken place. There were no debts, they said, because there had been no bets. So, all that money that he had set aside for paying them back, we have now for getting married. The wedding is going to be next autumn, when things slow down a little on the farm, and then we're going to buy our own house, and I can work part-time.'

While being of course extremely pleased at the *dénouement* of the episode, Cathy was not at all happy about the saga. 'You know, my dear,' she said, 'Max has had a close scrape with very unsavoury people. He has to accept that he has a problem.'

'Yes, I know that,' said Judy, looking frankly into Cathy's eyes. 'Once I got over being so happy that everything was going to be OK, I saw that he was going to need counselling to make sure it didn't happen again. In fact, I made it a condition of getting married. And he's already started.'

'Well, good for you. You're a very sensible young woman, and he's lucky to have you! I'm sure you'll be very happy together. Now, there, there,' Cathy said as Judy turned off the machine and a tear fell on the couch. 'These things do happen, and it could have been a lot worse.'

'Oh I know,' said Judy, wiping her eyes with her sleeve. 'It's just really good to be able to talk about it at last. I'm so sorry to have taken time from your session.'

'Now don't be silly. I feel better already,' said Cathy, kindly if untruthfully, as she reassembled herself. 'How much do I owe you?'

'This one's on me,' said Judy smiling and taking Cathy's hand. 'Only, it really is just between us . . .'

'I promised to keep your confidence, and I always keep my promises,' said Cathy, squeezing Judy's hand. 'Besides, it's not for me to spread what would only be malicious rumours. I will accept your kind gift of a free therapy session,' she continued with a twinkle, 'but only if you promise me a piece of the wedding cake.'

'It's a deal,' said Judy smiling, as she opened the door.

Now you will obviously be thinking that the fact that this episode is included in my narrative is evidence that Cathy did not in fact keep her word. And it is important to state that this is not at all the case. Throughout all the events that followed, Cathy gave no hint of Max's troubles to a soul, not even to her closest friends, until the facts came to light of their own accord. The nearest I came to apprehending that anything was amiss (and that was not very near), was that she used to grow thoughtful that December whenever I mentioned Judy or Max in her presence. But even this only became apparent to me with the benefit of hindsight. At the time, I was occupied with my own chiropractic appointments, which, if lacking the dramatic accoutrements of her physiotherapy sessions, nevertheless had an absorbing interest of their own.

And so it was that Christmas approached ever nearer, without any greater light being shed on Michael's murder. Everyone inevitably became taken up in preparations for the festive season, both privately and in terms of decorating the churches. Our Union of Parishes, which is in fact a Union of Unions, has, I am proud to say, a very good *esprit* and sense of working together for the common cause. At Christmas, it has been agreed to everyone's satisfaction, the services are spread round in a sensible and pleasant manner. Midnight Communion on Christmas Eve is always held in the pretty little country church at Noyestown, which lies at the opposite geographical extreme to Ardliss. Then on Christmas morning, at the usual Sunday time, there is a family Communion service at Greenborough, which is to the north of Ardliss, and rather nearer to Noyestown. There follows another family Communion service at Ardliss, also at the usual time of its Sunday service. There tend to be carol services as well at both the larger churches, which are ecumenical and well supported. So there is a lot to do to prepare the three churches to look their best, and each congregation takes an understandable pride in its church's appearance.

The little church of St Fechan's, Noyestown, is so picturesque that very little is needed to give it a warm, intimate feeling for Midnight Communion. Holly, fir branches, and candlelight are enough to awaken its magic. St Fechan's, Greenborough, by contrast, is an open rectangular shape with a high ceiling, originally designed more on the lines of a Dissenting meeting house. It therefore lends itself to more elaborate and large-scale decoration, with a Christmas tree and garlands, and holly wreaths, etc. But All Saints Ardliss is the largest and most imposing of the three. To decorate it requires a well-organised team effort. For most of

Advent there is nothing more than an Advent Wreath, placed in the Sanctuary. But for the Carol Service the tree will be up, and some of the holly and evergreen boughs. And by Christmas Day the pew decorations and flower arrangements will be in place. With Cathy out of action (except in a supervisory capacity), a more than ordinary share of this work fell to the rest of us. And what with this, our annual Christmas shoebox appeal, and our own private arrangements, I'm afraid that the mystery surrounding Michael's death gradually faded in our minds. In the busy run-up to the holiday, we in Ardliss were therefore ignorant for some time of the additional rumours that were circulating at the other end of the parish.

7
The Parish Newsletter

It was the third of December, and time for Beatrice Turner, the parish's Lay Pastoral Assistant, to bring parish newsletters to those who had not been able to come to church and collect their own. Because it was a bright, fair day, she decided to don her boots and take up her walking stick, and start her rounds by making an expedition to visit Herbert Greene. As she snaked through the steep, undulating hills and secret lakes that characterise the eastern side of the parish, she thought that she might do some shopping in Greenborough later on if she had time, since her visits would take her that way. After driving some distance she came upon a stretch of road that was darker than the rest, overhung with ancient holly, and ash trees smothered in ivy, that leant out over and through the remains of a long-rusted and semi-ruined gate. Here she pulled over, and parked her car as well as she could on the narrow, muddy verge. Examining the gate, she found it heavily padlocked. 'As if it would open anyway!' she thought to herself. She locked the car and, shouldering her bag, scrambled over the lowest portion of the ruined park wall, and let herself down on the other side. Soon she was immersed in the shadows of tall ivy-clad trees, and it was dark despite the sun in the sky. Picking her way along the rutted, muddy track, she caught an occasional glimpse of blue overhead between the towering Scots pine, and the beeches that characteristically still bore many curled, dry leaves. Their brittle rustling was the only sound, apart from the thin hissing of the wind through the pines.

As she struggled steeply uphill along the track, long since useless for vehicles, she reflected that despite the innumerable occasions upon which she had made this journey, it always surprised her how long it was. She stopped once or twice to catch her breath, and reflected that she was no longer as young as she had once been. Eventually she came round a bend where the track was just wide enough to make out — framed between ancient yews — the *façade* of a once-great house. It was now devoid of roof, windows, and many of its original crenellations, the remains of which lay about in heaps where they had fallen. Ivy and willow now grew out of the floors and through the window frames, and the only remaining inhabitants were a colony of endangered bats in the dining room, and a barn owl in the principal guest bedroom. Unsurprised at this sight, which Bea had of course fully anticipated, she made her way around the house, putting up a cock pheasant and several rabbits in the process, to the remains of the yard. Here there was a small modern bungalow, in poor repair, it is true, but with roof and windows intact. Smoke issued from the chimney and there was the smell of peat, so it was obvious that Herbert was in. 'Thank heavens for that,' Bea thought. 'I do hate coming all the way up here just to shove a newsletter under his door.' For the space under the door of the cottage did indeed form the only point of entry for letters; and they had to be thin ones, at that. Anything more substantial needed to be deposited on the front seat of the ruined car that stood in what had once been a stable.

'Herbie,' she called, knocking on the door. And it opened to reveal a small, pink, white-haired man with a pipe and a smile.

'Hello, hello, Bea,' he said, setting his Burke's *Peerage* on the cat's bed, where it remained opened at his favourite page. 'Come through to the fire. Will you have a cup of tea?'

I'd love one, Herbie. Here, I've brought you a newsletter. Where do you want it?'

'Stick it up over the last one behind the door if you wouldn't mind. What will you have, Assam, China, or Lapsang?'

Oh, Assam please. It's chilly enough, even with the sun. How have you been?'

'Oh, very well, really. Do you know, I've finally managed to persuade them that the park constitutes a wildlife habitat, and can count for REPS.'

'Well done! I must say you're ahead of us; we've only just been reading about the new REPS in the *Irish Farmers' Weekly*. What will you do with the arable this time?'

'I'm very tempted to try it in some of this new Finnish wheat that Helena has been telling me about. It's disease free, super-hardy, and the grain is as hard as you please. It's meant to make the best strong flour going.'

'It isn't GM, is it?' asked Bea dubiously.

'Good Lord, no! You wouldn't catch Helena dabbling with that sort of stuff, nor me, even if I got a license for it. It's like shooting yourself in the foot. No, it's just a great cross between standard cultivated wheat and an old primitive Finnish variety that's been rediscovered.'

'It's odd I haven't read anything about it,' said Bea.

'Ah, this is really cutting edge. I think that Helena was the first person in Ireland to hear of it; Will brought back news of it from one of his sub-Arctic safaris.'

'Well, you might let her have a go before committing yourself,' said Bea sensibly.

'Mm, I might, but then again I'd like to be out front with anything good that's going.'

They continued drinking in silence for a while, until Bea said, 'When are you going to repair the track and the gate, Herbie? You know it's crazy to have no access to the house by car.'

'I'm not having those damn' cowboys stealing any more of the house. I manage to get everything I need. It's a short walk across the meadow at the back to the main Greenborough road, and the bus is good.'

'But what if you were ill? How would an ambulance get to you?' asked Bea, returning to an oft-repeated theme.

'Well, I've got the phone. They could always land a helicopter in one of the fields if it was really serious. Haven't got Freya with you today?' he feinted, to draw the conversation away.

Bea forbore to comment that she could hardly have carried a Weimaraner over the park wall. In the same way, she decided not to point out that the last time she had brought a dog with her to visit him, it had been poisoned and had only just survived the experience. But from this reflection she said, 'You know Herbie, if the park is to be a wildlife habitat, you'll have to think twice about the rat poison.'

'Yes yes yes; I've already got rid of that. Extra cats in the barns. Here, you!' he exclaimed, looking towards the house cat's bed at this point and finding its inhabitant curled up on the *Peerage*. 'Off!' he said, retrieving the precious volume.

Sensing that the conversation was in decline, Bea thanked him for tea, and lifting her bag took her leave. 'You will let someone know if you need anything over the holiday, won't you?'

'Of course! Don't worry. I'll be out for Midnight anyway, I've got a lift. Where you off to now?'

'Oh, let me think,' said Bea. 'Greenborough, then as far as Noyestown, and back round by the bog. I'll take a shortcut back home past the lake.'

'Ah! Then try to find out about this development thing on the lake, won't you? I would very much like to know what's going on there.'

Stopping in her stride Bea turned and asked, '*Development*? What development? By the lake? What are they thinking of doing?'

'Well, that's what everyone would like to know,' said Herbie. 'It's *said* that Dickie Bird is part of a consortium planning to build a water-sports resort on the lake. You know the sort of thing; power boating, water skiing, that sort of thing. And presumably a sort of spa hotel and so on. I don't know; that's why it would be good if you could find out any more out about it.'

'*You can't possibly be serious*!' said Bea aghast. 'Lough Coile is one of the most famous fishing lakes in Ireland. And besides, it would destroy the whole character of the entire area! I can't believe that Dickie would do anything so horrid to all of us.'

'Mm, well, I hope not. Perhaps it's not him. Perhaps it's all a mare's nest anyway. But it would be good to know.'

'It would be more than good, it will be essential, if objections are to be lodged in time. You leave it with me. I will certainly get to the bottom of it, one way or another.' And thus Bea set out down the track with renewed purpose, reflecting, not for the first time, how often it was that by doing a good turn for someone else, one often benefits oneself.

I am sure that you will have no trouble believing that, on her subsequent visits, Bea was diligent in both raising the alarm and eliciting information. I am equally certain that you will not be surprised to learn that everyone on whom she called was as much in the dark as she herself. Eventually, in a fit of thwarted curiosity (as well as a genuine sense of urgency), she called at New Farm to see the younger Noyeses. They did not, of course, require either a newsletter or a pastoral visit. But they were the most likely people to know what was happening and to be concerned about it, being active in both farming and field sports locally. She was fortunate in finding Henry, who had just come in from inspecting his own REPS wildlife habitat. She lost no time in informing him of her concerns.

'I only heard the rumours yesterday,' he said, bringing her into the kitchen. 'But I've been down to check planning applications this morning, and the only thing they've received is a proposal to build a meditation centre on one of the islands on the lake. It's a crazy place to do it, if you ask me; what do they expect to do for power and clean water? Probably some New Age nonsense. But whoever it is (which I couldn't find out), has also applied to operate a small ferry to bring people on and off. The whole thing sounds bananas to me, but apparently they've already bought the island.'

'Well, it's obviously nothing Dickie Bird would be involved with,' said Bea, relieved.

'No,' said Henry doubtfully, 'That's as long as it's what it claims to be. But you know what planners can be like. It could be a toe in the water, with applications for amendments and additions to follow. And that *would* be like Dickie. The thing is, we're not going to find out anything more until after the New Year. So apart from keeping an ear to the ground, we'll just have to wait.'

And with that Bea had to be satisfied. 'It would probably be as well though to put as many people as possible on the lookout,' she reflected.

'Oh, absolutely;' Henry concurred. 'The more people there are keeping an eye out, the less likely it is that anything will slip past us.'

Reluctantly, Bea decided that she might as well do her shopping and then head home to tell her husband Frank what had transpired, and see if he had any further ideas to suggest. Returning to Greenborough, therefore, she parked her car in front of the church and walked the short distance to the supermarket. She quickly selected the items she had come for and joined a queue for checking out, only to find that she was standing behind Betty Lynne, another stalwart of the parish. Having greeted one another, Bea said, 'I've just heard from Henry Noyes that a planning application has been made for one of the islands in the lake to be turned into a *meditation* centre, whatever that is. It doesn't sound like anything Christian; that would surely be called a retreat centre; and besides, both parishes would know about it.'

'Perhaps it's something to do with all the Chinese people settling in Greenborough,' suggested Betty.

'Are there many Chinese people here?' asked Bea, surprised.

'Oh, yes,' Betty replied. 'All around in the new development. Haven't you seen the new Chinese Restaurant? I've heard it's quite good. And it's always packed with oriental people, which must be a good sign.'

'Of course; I keep walking past it without really noticing,' observed Bea. 'I hope it is good, because we could do with an alternative to the Greene Arms. I suppose,' she continued, 'that that's why there's a whole aisle here now devoted to Chinese food. I noticed it just now, and couldn't understand it; I assumed that Chinese food had become some new fashion.'

'Oh yes, it's for all the new families. There aren't many in here just at the moment,' said Betty looking round; 'they're usually here first thing. That's why there's never any broccoli or sweet peppers any more; you know how many vegetables go into Chinese food. I understand that the little charity shop that's closed is to be turned into an Asian market; I suppose that's why the supermarket is trying to get in first with the tinned and packeted stuff.'

'I wonder,' said Bea as Betty unloaded her basket at the till, 'whether we might get some new families. There might well be some Christians among them.'

'That would be great, wouldn't it?' agreed Betty. 'But I think they would most likely be Catholic, if there are any. I must ask Fr Eustace when I see him, whether he has any coming to his church. What would most Chinese be, though? If they've come here, they're hardly likely to be Communists.'

'Oh, no; I'm sure they'll be Buddhist mostly, from Singapore or Taiwan, or places like that. I wonder why on earth they want to come to Ireland?'

'Well, the economy is still booming; and Greenborough is considered to be in the Dublin commuter belt, though that seems crazy to me. Still,' continued Betty as she packed her bags and paid for her shopping, 'it should benefit the local economy too. Apart from doing their shopping here there's already a new noodle factory.'

'Is there really?' asked Bea, packing her own items as they came through the checkout. She was beginning to feel rather out of the loop for local intelligence.

'Oh yes, just out of Noyestown, along the bog road. It's either a factory or a distributor. It's in a warehouse along the track to the lake. You see the noodle lorry whizzing about; I'm sure there are other Chinese restaurants to supply as well as our new one.'

'Well,' said Bea collecting her bags, 'then the meditation centre might well be genuine, and something to do with the Chinese. What a relief! I wonder how Dickie Bird got involved with the rumour, or why a watersports centre was mentioned in the first place.'

'Oh, Dickie does want to have a watersports centre; I know that much from talking to him. But he'll never get planning for it. If the Chinese get their meditation centre up and running first, that should help scupper it, too.'

'If it *is* the Chinese who are planning the centre,' thought Bea as she said goodbye to Betty. What a roller-coaster day she was having. Whatever was going on, Henry was surely right in saying that it would not become clear until after the holidays. With her head in something of a spin, Bea now considered it to be more than time to return home to her own belated lunch. She had accomplished all her visits, and now felt rather tired. She therefore wound her car through the hills back to her own gate, and headed up the drive and over the cattle grids to the top of the little hill on which her own house sits. Standing for a moment to admire the lake below, she was greeted by a chorus of dogs, who rushed round from the back of the house scattering hens and peacocks in their wake. 'Yes, yes, I'm coming in now,' she replied to their excited yelps, as she took out her shopping bags and shut the car door with her boot. She hardly expected to find Frank at home; he would have had his own lunch and returned to the office of his organic feed business. But as she elbowed open the kitchen door she was pleased to find him there, in the midst of boiling the kettle and putting some fish fillets under the grill.

'Want some?' he asked, as she let the bags slump onto a chair and took her coat off.

'Oh, yes please. What a wonderful coincidence. I assumed you would have had lunch already,' she answered, setting places at the kitchen table as he put more fish under the grill.

'I would have, but I got hung up on the phone with a client. Have you had a good morning? You look rather tired.'

'Well, yes I suppose, the morning was successful;' she answered, heating the teapot. 'I got all the newsletters distributed, and the shopping done. I beat my way up to see Herbie Greene, and got the gossip there.'

'How is he?' asked Frank as Bea paused to rummage for tea bags.

'Oh, fine, just as usual. Is it true by the way that Helena has got permission to grow some new sort of GM wheat?'

'It's not GM at all!' replied Frank, appalled at the suggestion. 'Just a remarkable new hybrid. I believe that it's all sorted for her to be part of the trial here. I was talking to her earlier today at the butcher's, and you'll never guess what else she told me.'

'What's that?' asked Bea, happy to be diverted before launching into a description of the Lough Coile rumours.

'Apparently some film producer's PA rang up to ask if he could 'rent' the Abbey for a couple of months!'

'No! What a bizarre idea! I wonder why he hit upon them anyway? There must be all sorts of abbeys about for hire.'

'Heaven only knows,' said Frank with a chuckle. 'I would love to have heard her reply though.'

'Well, that's not the only gossip for today,' said Bea. And, putting her news in as succinct a form as possible while Frank served lunch, she poured the tea and waited for his reaction.

'But that's horrendous!' he said, taking his seat.

'I know,' she replied. 'Even if it is just the meditation centre, it ought to have been reported in the local press. I'm uneasy at the secrecy.'

'Exactly,' said Frank. 'And that's exactly what smells of Dickie Bird. Well, we shall have to be prepared to mobilise a protest the minute we hear anything definite.'

'Yes,' said Bea. 'Henry doesn't think anything will happen until after Christmas.'

'No, probably not,' agreed Frank, stirring his tea thoughtfully. 'We'll just have to try to put it out of our minds until the new year.'

But they were both only too aware of how difficult everyone would find that to do.

J.E. RUTHERFORD

8
The Noyes Watercolours

As the season of Advent advanced, Matthew Carrington started to make his rounds bringing Communion to the housebound for Christmas. Things at this time of year are always so hectic that if he were to postpone his start until the week before Christmas, there would inevitably be some people left to be visited in the period between Christmas Day and Epiphany. And although this would actually be more correct (in terms of the lectionary) than starting Christmas in Advent, it is not so popular among the recipients. It thus transpired that the Monday after the third Sunday of Advent Matthew set out from the Rectory to visit Wendy Noyes, youngest surviving child of Admiral Noyes, hero of the Great War. Turning right from the Rectory gate, he reached the square of Ardliss and then turned sharply left, past the supermarket and the bungalows, farms and meadows, until, twisting steeply downhill around the ruins of an ancient church, he arrived on the bog. Here he had to be attentive. Even on a clear day, the flat expanse of the bog is confusing, in terms of both directional bearings and distances. There were three or four roads within the first few miles that turned suddenly north, to his right. All are private lanes that lead to farms, except the one that qualifies as a real road, since it goes through to Noyestown. They are all of them nearly invisible until one is on top of them, or indeed past them.

THE SERPENT IN THE GARDEN

Matthew had learnt to identify the road to Noyestown by a brown heritage sign on the main road, indicating the way to Lough Coile; but for some reason it was no longer in place. He therefore kept a careful lookout.

Like so many bog and moorland roads, this one is little more than single-track, with occasional wide spots to enable cars coming from opposite directions to pass each other. And so it was with a degree of irritation that Matthew found himself behind a *Fishy Business* van, that was itself held up behind a lorry bearing the name *Nippon Noodles*. 'There really is too much development being allowed,' he thought to himself. So much of rural Ireland seemed to have been spoilt already by sprawling development with no social infrastructure. He could not honestly say that that had happened yet in Ardliss, Greenborough, or Noyestown, but it loomed on local consciousness as an ever-present threat. The very idea of a noodle factory being allowed on this vast, beautiful bog seemed to him outrageous. Sure enough, in confirmation of his suspicions, the lorry turned off not far from Noyestown, at a junction indicating the road to Lough Coile. At least there was no delay now, as the fish van sped along with the confidence of familiarity, and Matthew found himself following it all the way to Wendy's small house, where they both stopped.

'Hello, Declan,' said Matthew. 'Bringing an order for Miss Noyes?'

'That's just it,' said Declan, emerging with a smile. 'She's very fond of the salmon and trout fillets, especially. Very convenient to have in the freezer, especially if you're only wanting one or two at a time.

'Hello, Miss Noyes,' he said, turning to the elderly lady who had emerged smiling at the door of the house; 'A box of salmon and a box of trout, isn't that it? Don't come down, sure I'll bring them up to you.'

As Wendy found her purse and Declan wrote out his receipt, Matthew said conversationally, 'It's a nuisance having these noodle lorries all over the bog, isn't it? I'm amazed anyone was given planning permission for a factory in a place of such natural beauty, especially given the proximity to Lough Coile.'

'Oh, I don't think it's a factory; I'm sure it isn't,' replied Declan, removing Wendy's copy of the receipt and setting it on her hall table. 'I'm sure it's just a distributor. They're in that old warehouse that used to be kept for farm machinery parts. If they're just a distributor they wouldn't need planning, and to be honest with you I think it's better to have the warehouse in use than standing idle. I dare say the rent is cheap. And I don't see the lorries that often. I don't think it's a big set-up.'

'Oh, well, that's not so bad, then. I suppose we're all becoming rather jittery about any more development, given all the new housing in Greenborough, and Ardliss; even some in Noyestown.'

'Oh, I know that; mind you, I'm happy enough with that development in Greenborough. It's not just noodles these Chinese people eat! I sell more fish now in that one development than I used to in the whole of the

County. And I supply the Chinese Restaurant too. Have you tried it? The food is beautiful. Though I must say the sauces were a bit spicy for my liking.'

'What's this?' asked Wendy, reappearing with her purse and counting out exact change for Declan.

'Declan's been singing the praises of this new Chinese Restaurant. Have you been yet?'

'I have!' said Wendy. 'We had a pensioners' lunch there recently as a Christmas outing, and it really was very good. Full of Chinese people, too, which is always a good sign.'

'I'll just put these in the freezer for you,' said Declan, putting his books away.

'I'll take them for you, really,' said Matthew; 'I'm coming in anyway.'

'Fair enough; thank you Rector. Tell your wife when you see her that I haven't forgotten that snapper for her. She'll have it in good time for Christmas, say Wednesday or Thursday. Good day to you both,' and in a twinkling he was gone.

'Here, let's get these into the freezer for you,' said Matthew, as he and Wendy went into the house. 'How have you been? It's such a pity that you won't be out for Christmas; though it's good that you can get in for the tests before the holidays. When do you go?'

'Tomorrow. There is *just* the chance that I'll be out again for Christmas, but even if I am I'll have to stay with Tom and Sarah, and I don't know that I'll be up to going out. It's very good of you to come today.'

'Not at all,' said Matthew as they went into the sitting room and he prepared for the service.

It is Matthew's custom to stay for a cup of tea and a chat after officiating at a home Communion, as it is a social occasion for the housebound.

'Shall I put the kettle on?' asked Matthew as he and Wendy moved together towards the kitchen.

'Please, if you don't mind,' said Wendy.

As they stepped together into the hall, Matthew's attention was struck by a lovely watercolour of a Scottish lake and castle, with mountains in the background.

'Goodness,' said Matthew, feeling a sudden nostalgia for home, 'I'd never noticed this before. It's lovely.'

'I've only recently put it there,' said Wendy. 'Do you think it's a good place for it? It's one of my great-grandmother's, my mother's grandmother. She was a very good artist, very well trained, but of course in those days it was only really respectable for ladies to do watercolours. I think she would have done very good oil portraits, like Gwen John perhaps, or Berthe Morisot. But it wouldn't really have been acceptable in those days for a gentlewoman. Her still lifes and landscapes are still very fresh today, though, don't you think?'

'Absolutely. This is beautiful. Do you know where it is? It reminds me of my home in Perthshire.'

'I'm sorry, I don't. Great-grandmama's family home was in Fife, though, so it could well be. Would you like to see the others? I've brought them down into the dining room.'

'If you're sure you don't mind, I'd love to,' said Matthew.

Leading the way into the dining room, therefore, Wendy turned on the light, and Matthew gasped. Crowded on all the walls, nearly from floor to ceiling, were exquisite paintings of Scottish and Irish scenes, and still lifes of flowers and fruit, and a few of game bags with rabbits, grouse and pheasants. Unlike the usual modest, tentative, and frankly watery products of artistically inclined Georgian and Regency ladies, however, there was a richness in the colouring and a bold economy in the brush work that was masterful, and spoke of real talent.

'I've only seen such vivid colours in watercolours before in the Turner collection,' said Matthew.

'Oh, yes, Great-grandmama was a committed devotee of Mr Turner. As a matter of fact, although women artists were not of course taken very seriously then, she received a letter from him praising her work. She kept it, of course. It's around the house somewhere. I inherited all her things, since she left them through the female line, unusually.'

Do you know,' said Matthew, wandering about the room in a daze, 'I'm not sure that you should really have them all hanging together in the house like this. I've a feeling that they're very valuable.'

'Yes, of course, I know;' said Wendy. 'That's just what Richard Bird told me. I don't know how it was that he heard of them, but he called one day and asked to see them. And really I'm afraid I hadn't thought of them for years. They've been hanging about upstairs, and stacked in the attic. It was he who brought them down for me. I could never have done it myself. And he hung them downstairs, and took an inventory. Really it was very kind of him, and took him a great deal of time. Once I saw them all and remembered how many there are, and how really very good, I could see at once that he was right.'

'Right about what?' asked Matthew.

'Oh, he told me, just as you have, that they shouldn't be left in the house like this. So, he very cleverly suggested that he could have them taken away and copied, so that I could have the copies at home. The originals can then be kept safe in the bank, or somewhere. He'll have them valued for me, and then they can be put away safely. Not that the valuation is important to me. There are no girl children to leave them to, so they'll revert to the National Art Museum. It really is extraordinarily kind of him to take the trouble. I couldn't thank him enough when he offered, it will be such a weight off my mind. But he told me that he's a lover of art, and that he's only too happy to help.'

'Oh, certainly,' said Matthew, unsure how to respond to this. 'Well, I know that Angela would love to see them before they go.'

'Of course, she must call and see them. Once they're in the museum of course they will be easy to see, and better hung and lit. But I don't intend to pop off for a while yet,' Wendy remarked with a smile and a twinkle in her eye. 'Now, is it tea of coffee that you would like?'

And so the conversation reverted to more mundane things, as Matthew was regaled with mince pies and water-sports gossip. But as he prepared to take his leave, Wendy said, 'And perhaps if you see Richard you might remind him that he is to come and take the paintings away. I think that I shall feel easier when they are gone.'

'I shall certainly do that,' said Matthew, not displeased to be given an excuse to quizz Dickie about the whole business. 'I should be seeing him later tonight at the concert at the Abbey.'

Matthew's mind was, not surprisingly, full of all these things, as well as of the visits he was still to make that day, when he approached the turning towards the lake and noodle distributor. 'There's Declan again,' he thought to himself; he flashed his lights at the *Fishy Business* van that zoomed out from the lake road and turned in front of him. 'The distributor must live over the shop. I wonder how Declan will get all his Christmas deliveries made, criss-crossing about like that. I must remember to give his message to Angela.'

'Oh, by the way, Declan said he would have your order for you on Wednesday or Thursday,' Matthew said virtuously, as he and Angela dressed for the Christmas Concert at the Abbey.

'Oh good. I was getting a little anxious. Where did you see him?'

'Up at Wendy's. He certainly seems to have a lot of business. Apparently the Chinese people in the new development at Greenborough eat vast quantities of his fish. I think he's pushed doing his rounds these days.'

'He is,' agreed Angela. 'I've heard that he's had to divide his territory and let someone else have a bit because he's so in demand.'

'Well, that's a nice problem to have. That explains why he didn't go to the noodle distributor on the way up to Wendy. The bog must be part of the new fellow's remit.'

'You mean you've found out more about the famous noodle factory?' asked Angela with interest. 'How big is it? They say it's going to employ a hundred people, and that they're going to have to build a new road to take the lorries.'

'Ha!' said Matthew. 'So much for rumours. That's just the like of people. It's not a factory at all, just a distributor, and I don't think it's got more than a couple of lorries. Declan knew all about it.'

'Well, I'm glad someone knows something about something. You didn't hear any more about the water sports centre?'

'No,' said Matthew. 'Wendy had heard about it, but couldn't credit that the County Council would allow anything that would spoil the fishing. And really that does make sense. It probably is a meditation centre, after all. How're we doing for time? What are we hearing tonight, by the way? I hope it isn't more *Lieder*.'

'No, it's the Morgenstern Quartet, Mozart and Schubert.'

'Well, that sounds good.'

THE SERPENT IN THE GARDEN

And so it was that the Carringtons set out for the concert before Matthew had had a chance to tell Angela about Wendy's watercolour collection. Concerts at the Abbey take place in the Great Hall, with refreshments available in the dining room during the interval. This is generally characterised by a scrum as people struggle to join the respective queues for tea or wine. *Cognoscenti* are adept at ensuring they join the appropriate queue without getting entangled in the other, but there is always a degree of confusion, exacerbated by the monumental dining table in the middle of the room. It was while insinuating themselves into the wine queue that the Carringtons discovered themselves in the vicinity of Dickie Bird, and Matthew remembered his message.

'Ah, Dickie;' he said. 'I've a message for you from Wendy Noyes about her great-grandmother's watercolours.'

At this Dickie smiled in a rather too-natural way, and, his eyes having darted about rapidly, said,' Ah yes; pretty little things, aren't they?'

'More than pretty, surely,' said Matthew. 'I was staggered by them. A woman with that amount of talent would be a household name these days, great lady or no.'

'What's this?' said Angela with interest.

'Aye, Wendy Noyes's mother's mother's mother did incredible watercolour landscapes and still lifes. I saw them today. Masses of them. And they aren't just your genteel daubs. The colours are luminous. You would love them. You have an invitation to see them.'

'Yes, they are rather good of their kind, but you know the world is littered with ladies' watercolours,' said Dickie.

'But that's just what I'm saying! Any woman who corresponded with Turner and had his compliments had to be something out of the ordinary.'

'*What?*' said Angela.

'This is what I'm trying to tell you,' said Matthew with a hint of exasperation. 'And you yourself, Dickie, told Wendy that they were too valuable to have in the house, as indeed they must be. It makes me a little nervy to think of her sitting there with something over a hundred of them.'

'*A hundred?*' said Angela.

By this time, everyone around them was listening with interest. Before Matthew had a chance to continue, however, Dickie said, 'Yes, of course they're fine as watercolours go, but I was also trying to be polite in my praise of them.'

'Well,' said Matthew, 'it was certainly very good of you to bring them down from the attic for her. And you must have a reasonably good opinion of them since you've offered to take them away for copying so that the originals can be put in safe keeping.'

At this point all eyes were on Dickie, and he stepped back a pace involuntarily. In doing so he inadvertently trod on Mr Moto (who was inclined to get rather lost in the undergrowth at these events). Mr Moto squeaked, and Dickie jumped, and it would all have been quite farcical, except that something about Dickie's expression lent gravitas to the scene. 'Sorry, Moto, old fellow,' said Dickie. 'Yes, well, one likes to be of help to the elderly, you know. And as you say, they are quite nice little paintings. Thank you so much,' he turned and took his glass of wine, and with a smile moved off and was swallowed up in the crowd.

'What on earth was that all about?' asked Angela, as she and Matthew received their glasses in their turn.

'Well, I'm not entirely sure, now,' said Matthew. 'I'll tell you more later. We'd better drink these and circulate, because the interval will soon be over.'

As there was no more to be got from Matthew on the subject, there was nothing for Angela to do but try to put it all to the back of her mind for the time being. Matthew had begun speaking to an elderly couple from the parish, who were rather hard of hearing, and Angela cast her eyes about to see who was near her.

'Hello!' said an effervescent voice behind her.

Turning with a smile, Angela said, 'Hello, John! I didn't know you were here tonight. Is Betty with you? It's a long way to come from Greenborough.' The Lynnes were only able to attend concerts now and again, both because of the distance from Greenborough, and also because Betty still worked part-time as a nurse, and sometimes her hours prevented it.

'Oh, yes,' said John; 'over there, talking with Bea Turner. We were able to come to this concert because it was on a Monday. Very unusual, isn't it? I really didn't think many people would be here. It's a very good night for us, but not for most people. But what a crowd!'

'Yes, I think everyone has made a real effort for the Morgenstern Quartet. It's incredible to think of them playing here. But of course the Abbey is now part of the international music scene, thanks to William and Helena — and of course the Turners.'

'Quite,' said John. 'And I suppose that any time in the week before Christmas would be a draw; people will be out at things every night. How on earth did we get Morgenstern?'

'They're on their way to America somewhere, and had a couple of days between airports. Yes, we really are lucky, especially at this time of year. I'm glad they've got a good appreciative crowd for their efforts.'

'Indeed. I'm looking forward to the Schubert. It's really what we're here for,' said John.

'Yes, I think that's true for most of us. It's so difficult to get expression into Mozart, isn't it?'

'I suppose it is; I hadn't really thought about it.'

'I was meaning to speak to you or Betty to say how very kind it is to have us in for lunch on Sunday,' said Angela. 'Are you really sure you want us? Christmas Eve is such a busy time.'

'It's busier for Matthew than for us! Yes, of course, we're looking forward to it. The children only arrive in Christmas week, so we're taking the opportunity of Christmas Eve to Boxing Day to have our own friends in for a change.'

'Well, it's very kind of you, and we really are looking forward to it.'

'It's a bit awkward for you, though, isn't it? We hadn't really thought, but you'll have to come back up from Ardliss, and then go home, and then come back to Noyestown for Midnight.'

'That's no trouble, really. Matthew's so used to driving around the parish now that he just goes on autopilot.'

The gong sounded the end of the interval; glasses were relinquished and seats regained. And it would wait until Sunday, Christmas Eve, for Angela to discover just how eventful driving about the parish could be.

9

Christmas Eve

'It's curious, isn't it,' said Angela to Matthew as they gathered up their gifts and got into the car. 'You would think that having Christmas Eve on a Sunday might make things easier, but really it's the worst day of all. You still have to do your Sunday services, but then the three Christmas ones follow straight on.'

'Well, at least I was able to have this morning's celebrations as 'said' services with no address,' replied Matthew. 'But it's true; I suppose that Christmas on Sunday is best. I'd be doing the morning services anyway, so it would only be Midnight in addition. But somehow it's always a marathon, no matter what day it is!'

'I know! At least this year we're having a special Christmas Eve dinner, thanks to the Lynnes, rather than just collapsing between services!'

It's really nice of them, isn't it? And although it makes a long day today, we'd really be too tired to make something special just for ourselves.'

'Yes;' replied Angela. 'We'll end up going back into collapse mode tomorrow!' It is the Carringtons' custom to observe their own Christmas festivities on the twelfth day of the season (Epiphany), since they are always too tired to do so in the period immediately before or after the day itself. Not having children, they had found that observation of the traditional seasonal rituals had tended gradually to slip away. And so it was with a particularly festive feeling that they made their way to the Lynnes' that day. The weather was bright and frosty; and quite suddenly, as frequently happens to people at this time of year, they felt it to be Christmastide.

'I wonder who else will be there?' Angela mused.

'I gather it will be the Turners, and the younger Noyeses.'

'Oh, that's nice; very 'ecumenical': representatives of all three congregations!' said Angela.

'There's a really good spirit in the parish among the three churches; we're lucky.'

'Where's something wooden?' Angela asked, rapping Matthew on the top of his head. 'Don't tempt fate!'

'That's superstition!' laughed Matthew. 'Oh, blast!'

'What's the matter?' asked Angela. They had by now turned off the main bog road and onto the one leading to Noyestown.

'It's that wretched noodle lorry again. On a Sunday! On Christmas Eve! Who needs noodles on Christmas Eve?'

'Perhaps it's going to the Lynnes',' said Angela irrepressibly. 'We might be going to have noodles and fish for lunch. Declan has probably already called!'

'I suppose it's just being taken back to the warehouse for the holidays. The whole of the midlands must be full of noodles by now!'

'I'm sure it won't be just noodles that they deliver,' observed Angela *en gourmande.* 'Which part of China is it again that eats noodles? I can never remember. There's a sort of 'noodle line' in China. On one side everyone eats rice, and on the other, noodles.'

'Well, the ones in Greenborough obviously come from the noodle side,' observed Matthew. 'Yes, sure enough, there he goes towards the warehouse.'

They drove on straight for a few minutes, and then, turning right before reaching Noyestown, they soon saw before them the symmetrical mound that characterises the Lynnes' house, Lisrath. This ancient earthwork, of uncertain original purpose, lies in the front garden of the present house. It is reputed to mark an entrance to the fairy kingdom, but if so, none of the Lynnes had ever encountered any of that realm's subjects, much to the disappointment of successive generations of children. Pulling up before the front door, the Carringtons saw that the Turners and the Noyeses had already arrived.

'Come in, come in!' said Betty, opening the door to them. She was wearing a beautiful purple cashmere sweater above her tweed skirt, and a simple strand of pearls. 'Happy Christmas! We're starting it early. Just consider it the run-up to Midnight.' Having divested themselves of their coats, Betty led them into the conservatory. 'We're having sherry in here; I think it's warm enough, don't you? What a difference the sun makes.'

There were greetings all round, and the Carringtons handed Betty their offerings. 'Oh, thank you! I'll put them under the tree; John will get you something to drink.'

They were soon immersed in the party, and Matthew found himself standing next to Henry Noyes. 'How are you? I haven't seen you for awhile. Have you been away?' he asked.

'No, unfortunately. We decided to try doing organic turkeys this year and it's been a nightmare. We only just got the last ones delivered this morning before we came here! And Linda's shop is doing really well, so I haven't had her around to help.'

'Well, but that's a nice thing to complain of! I see Angela talking to her now; that looks dangerous. She really loves the things Linda gets in.'

'Well, fortunately a lot of people seem to! She's going to start doing some clothes, too, not just handbags and jewelry. Just to test the water. Some coats and sweaters. She got a few in for Christmas and they disappeared in three days!'

'Well, I'm hardly surprised! It's not easy to get dressed here without ending up in a sweater and a coat; she might try gum boots as well!'

'Don't, please!' said Henry seriously. 'She's got a catalogue with all sorts of designer wellies; floral, check, leather trimmed, you name it.'

'I don't think fancy things like that would last long around here,' said Matthew.

'Well, I suppose they'd be OK for shopping or collecting the kids from school,' mused Henry.

'Dear, dear! Anyone would think we lived in the suburbs. The next thing you know people will be buying these SUVs.'

'You both look rather serious!' said Frank Turner coming up to them. 'Not conspiring against the speed boats are you?'

'Oh, don't!' they both groaned.

'I'm trying to forget about rumours until the middle of January,' said Henry.

'I know,' said Frank ruefully; 'but it's not easy, is it? I can be in the middle of doing something completely different, and suddenly some thought will strike me. Like, where would the road be for the traffic? And the parking? I don't know where the resort or club house or whatever it is would be.'

'Well, the road's easy;' said Henry. 'It would have to be the one that goes past the noodle warehouse. That's the only one that goes straight to the lake, unless they got permission to make an entirely new one; and that costs money. There's a bit of parking down there already, and a couple of slips for boats.'

'You know,' said Matthew, 'in a way that noodle warehouse is a good omen. It makes me feel that there really is some sort of meditation centre on the cards. It stand to reason that the new Chinese community would want some sort of centre of that kind; and if a Chinese firm has already started a business down there, it could well be the beginning of something more, like a catering company.'

THE SERPENT IN THE GARDEN

With this happy surmise the conversation shifted, and circulated, as is the way of such gatherings. Soon the company was called to the table, and, grace said, fell to the serious business of appreciating their lunch. It was only with the appearance and distribution of the flaming pudding that conversation became more general again. And with the discovery of the sixpence by Linda Noyes (it was a real one, recycled by Betty every year for luck), seasonal jollity bubbled over, and they all found themselves, despite however many solemn resolutions made beforehand, wearing paper hats and reading out silly jokes to one another.

'Coffee in the conservatory!' said Betty, removing plates. And so they all moved off, and once furnished with brandy etc assembled round the fire in the morning room, from which the conservatory extends. Even confirmed standers ended up sitting comfortably in armchairs, and, coffee poured and chocolates passed, John said 'Now for presents!'

'Oh, you're not doing presents, are you?' asked Linda.

'Of course!' said John. 'It's Christmas — just a little early. You've all brought us presents, and we have something for each of you.'

'What a lovely day,' said Bea to Angela, as everyone laughed, or gasped, or whatever was most appropriate to their gift. At last, everyone had received something except Matthew, and there was nothing left under the tree.

'And now, Matthew,' said John, 'I'm afraid you're going to have to come into the kitchen for your present.'

'And everyone is to ignore the mess!' said Betty.

With eager curiosity the company followed a bemused Matthew to the kitchen. 'Now, this isn't really from us. It's from Angela to you, but we've been keeping it for her until today.'

Coming into the kitchen, Matthew was taken to the far side of the Aga, where there was what appeared to be a box, covered with a table cloth. As everyone crowded round, furtive rustling noises came from within. Matthew cast a 'What have you been up to?' glance at Angela, who was careful to remain at the back of the throng. Then, carefully lifting the cloth, he found a small cage with a tiny, one-eyed terrier puppy sitting in the middle, its little tail wagging as it looked up at him with its head cocked.

'Aaah!' came the chorus from behind him.

'You've been saying that you wanted a little dog to go about with you on your visits,' said Angela.

The little creature was as adorable as all baby animals are; and particularly all Jack Russell puppies.

'When I went to look at the litter he was the only one left. No one wanted him because of his eye. He lost it when he was only four weeks old. I couldn't just leave him there,' said Angela, rather predictably.

The little fellow came up towards Matthew and stood up against the railings of the cage, still wagging his tiny tail. What could he do? Reaching in Matthew took him out and held him close, and was rewarded with a nuzzle and a lick on the face. The deed was done. The little fellow started nibbling Matthew's fingers with his tiny puppy teeth.

'Ah, Agrippa!' Matthew said.

'What?' said John.

'That's his name!'

'How are we going to look after him?' Matthew asked Angela rather peevishly on their way home.

'*I'm* going to look after him, until he's old enough to go out with you. I've got everything ready for him at home, and I've read up all about them.'

'It will be a lot of work,' he said.

'But I work from home; he will keep me company. Don't worry! I thought you wanted one!'

'I do, but Christmas is such a busy time!'

'Oh, just enjoy it,' said Angela, as the new baby of the family nuzzled his face further under her arm. 'I've even got him a Christmas stocking of his own.'

And so the newly constituted family wended its way across the bog on the way home. 'It will nearly be true that lunch was the first part of the Midnight service!' observed Matthew. It was six o'clock, and the frost of the day had turned into a softly rising mist from the evening shadows of the bog.

'Good Lord! What on earth is that?' Matthew said suddenly, startling Angela from a doze. Ahead of them and to the left, out on the bog, the shifting mist intermittently revealed the shape of a long rectangular vehicle of some sort. As they strained their eyes to make out what it might be, they saw two figures emerging from the back of it, bearing between them a long, shallow box.

Before they could make out any more, they were past the spot. 'That looked exactly like . . .' started Matthew;

'Don't say it!' said Angela. 'How really weird. Creepy. What on earth are two men doing on Christmas Eve depositing coffins on the bog!'

'Now *you* said it,' said Matthew. There was a soft whimpering sound from Angela's armpit.

'Shh!' she said. 'We're upsetting Agrippa.'

'But really,' Matthew continued in more subdued tones, 'I wonder what on earth that was about. It couldn't be turf cutters.'

'It was people dumping stuff that the bin men won't take,' said Angela sensibly, protectively cradling the infant Agrippa.

'On Christmas Eve? In the dark?' Matthew countered. But to these observations neither of them could think of a reply.

Once back home, the first priority was to settle Agrippa into his new house. His cage was duly set beside their own Aga, with his own little bed and baby-sized hot water bottle. Unsettled by the move from the Lynnes', he curled himself into the water bottle, tucked his head under it, and went to sleep. 'Well, that's him settled for the night,' said Angela in a whisper as they tiptoed out of the kitchen. 'I assume you weren't expecting anything else to eat this evening!'

'Don't even mention the idea!' said Matthew. 'All I want now is a couple of hours' sleep before we have to leave again.'

Three hours' sleep never feels adequate after a full morning's work and a full afternoon's entertainment. It also runs contrary to most peoples' habits to dress to go out at eleven o'clock in the evening. It was therefore with rather an effort of will that the Carringtons wrapped themselves up to face the chill of the night, and the drive before them. Taking a fond look at little Agrippa before departing, they were soon off again to Noyestown. 'I'm going to keep an eye out for that thing on the way up,' said Matthew. 'Can you remember where it was exactly?'

'I can never remember where anything is on the bog exactly, even in daylight,' replied Angela. 'I only know that it was between the Lynnes' and the main road. I would say about half way, but I was dozing.'

'Yes,' said Matthew; 'it was after the twisty bit, on the long straight stretch. That doesn't help much.'

'There are some tracks onto the bog that the turf cutters use,' observed Angela, 'but you can't tell at night where exactly they are.'

'No; the thing just seemed to be in the middle of the bog, with no visible means of having driven there. I wish now that I'd stopped to see what exactly it was.'

'I'm very glad you didn't!' said Angela. 'You would just have ended up falling into a cutting and breaking your leg.'

Despite their best efforts, they were able to discern no evidence at all of either the vehicle or its occupants on their drive to the church.

'Did you think that it was motorised?' asked Angela once they were well past where the apparition must have been. 'I didn't see any horses.'

'No,' agreed Matthew; 'but then I didn't see a driver's cab where you would expect it, either. I suppose it might have been a wagon of some sort.'

But soon they were drawing up at the little church of St Fechan's, Noyestown, and they had to put the mystery to the backs of their minds. The windows were glowing with candle light, and the moon cast shadows from the yews onto the silvery sparkle of frosty grass. People were walking up the path in twos and threes, and as they reached the light flowing from the open door, their frozen breath was visible. The harmonium was playing *Silent Night*, the stars were as bright as tiny spotlights, and two curious horses had wandered out into their paddock next door and stood surveying the scene. Grabbing his case, Matthew went on ahead of Angela to prepare for the service, while she parked the car and followed at a more leisurely pace. Walking up the path, she was overtaken by cheerful greetings, and found that it was the Lynnes. 'Time for the next course!' said Betty. 'This time we're the guests.' And indeed the entire lunch party (with the exception of Agrippa) was reassembled in the church, the Turners having come from nearly as far afield as the Carringtons. Henry Noyes was ringing the bell, which tolled clearly in the night. The church was full; a warm, happy phenomenon that only happens a couple of times a year, or else for weddings and funerals. And as Angela took her place and opened her hymn book for the first hymn, the feeling swept over her that they really were in the best of all possible parishes, if not in the best of all possible worlds.

By the time the service was finishing, the last verse of *O Come All Ye Faithful* filling the church, the infectious magic of Christmas had worked its spell. No one rushed to leave; rather, the aisle was filled with people chatting over the strains of *Hark, the Herald Angels Sing*. In the vestry Matthew was laughing with the two church wardens, Henry and Sylvia, as they counted the collection and completed the register. It was more to reassure himself, than to initiate gossip, that he said, 'I don't suppose either of you knows why someone would be out on the bog earlier this evening burying boxes.'

Suddenly, the laughter stopped. '*Burying boxes*?' said Henry.

'Sure why would anyone be out on the bog on Christmas Eve at all, let alone burying things,' asked Sylvia. 'When was this?'

'Well, I don't know;' said Matthew. 'It seemed rather odd to us. It was about six o'clock this evening, as we were coming home from the Lynnes' after lunch.'

'Oh, if it was coming home after the party, that explains it!' said Henry, rallying. The sounds of the departing congregation swept along beside them, and various people popped their heads in to say 'Merry Christmas!' The subject would have dropped there, but the parish Treasurer came into the vestry, and Sylvia asked him, 'You wouldn't know why someone would be out on the bog tonight burying crates, would you?'

'Not crates, exactly;' Matthew corrected her. 'More long and shallow,' and he indicated the shape of the box as best as he could remember it, with his hands.

'That looks like a coffin!' observed the Treasurer. 'In the bad old days I suppose it would be guns they would have been hiding. But these days I can't think what it would be. Are you sure they buried it?'

'That's just it,' said Matthew; 'we were past before we saw what they were doing with it, but they definitely took it out of the vehicle and carried it out onto the bog.'

'Well, that's peculiar. It wasn't a tractor, was it? Maybe someone was just dumping things illegally.'

'That's what Angela thinks,' admitted Matthew. 'But it definitely wasn't a tractor.'

'Well, that is strange,' agreed the Treasurer, and Henry and Sylvia thought so too.

'I'd keep an eye out, if I were you,' said Henry. 'If you see anything more it might be worth reporting, though I don't know what anyone could do about it.'

The subject seemingly exhausted at this point, conversation reverted to more appropriate themes. The question of the box was overtaken by holiday spirit. But neither Henry nor Sylvia had made light of the affair, as Matthew had hoped they would; nor indeed had the Treasurer. The whole thing seemed odd and unpleasant, despite Matthew's conviction that it must have some mundane explanation. Coming out to the car and seeing Angela laughing happily with the organist, he decided not to speak about it again on the way home. Why spoil the happiness of the season? But it *was* odd. That thought kept coming back to him, and over the holiday he was aware of it as a nagging presence somewhere in the farther reaches of his consciousness.

10
St Stephen's Day

Boxing Day arrived, in the midst of a period of wind, sleet and fog. It was with difficulty that we were able to work up any seasonal cheerfulness, though the spirit at church on Christmas Day had been pleasant enough. But at the Abbey, there was no avoiding being aware of the weather. The huge Christmas tree that stood in the outer courtyard moaned in the wind, its decorations sighing and fluttering. The Avakians had gone home for the holidays, or at least to see relatives and friends in eastern Europe, and wouldn't be back until after Orthodox Christmas (Epiphany to you and me). Claudia Crespi was of course at home with her family, and Mr Moto had left just that morning to return home for a few weeks. He had faithfully attended the solstice at Newgrange (having had luck in the draw for places), and after spending Christmas day among us had now departed. Cathy had kindly invited him, together with Mark Charles, Penny and myself, to Christmas dinner in her apartment, and I must say that she succeeded in making a very jolly party of it. For the first time since I could remember, there was laughter and banter. Cathy and I had prepared a very traditional Christmas dinner (with Mr Moto especially in mind) complete with flaming brandy on the pudding, which had a euro coin hidden in it. We had crackers, and a small gift for everyone, and it was all very homely. We had found a lovely, beautifully painted metal 'toy soldier' Crusader for Mr Moto, and it was evident, despite cultural differences, that he was genuinely touched. Cathy has a small upright piano, and we had ended up around it singing Christmas carols while Mark played for us, sipping our coffee and brandy in the warmth of the fire, as the wind howled outside. It was only after the others had left, as I was helping Cathy clear up, that I had come across the little present that she had obviously prepared for Dickie.

'What a pity Dickie didn't come,' I said. 'I haven't seen him about for a while. Is he away again?'

'I saw him at the concert last week, and I had thought he said he would be here. On the other hand I know he was to go off at some point, I think to Indonesia, to have tooth implants. He had mentioned that he was going sometime this winter. We both know how unpredictable he is; I deliberately got something that wouldn't go to waste,' she said, pulling the wrapping off to reveal a small bottle of good port. 'We can have it as a night-cap, to keep the chill out!'

'Tooth implants, eh?' I said, as we sipped the port and bundled dishes and glasses into the dishwasher. 'Aren't they very expensive? I'm sure that they're cheaper in Indonesia, but even so.'

'I get the impression, not from anything he's said, mind you, that Dickie is doing rather well of late. I believe that he's sold his interest in that field, but I don't know who to,' replied Cathy.

'I hope that means an end to this housing development plan, at any rate,' I observed. 'I always thought that was rather wild.'

'Well, let's hope so,' said Cathy. 'From talking with Sinead, I gather that she's keen to try putting it to this marvellous new hybridised wheat everyone's talking about. But I can't see that it could pay much if anything, for several years at least. It's an awfully scruffy field, and would take a good deal of preparation.'

'Oh well,' I observed, 'only time will tell.'

And so it was that, with Mr Moto, Claudia, the Avakians, and Dickie away, we were a diminished group who met the following evening in the Abbey library for the little sherry party that Helena traditionally gives on St Stephen's Day for the courtyard tenants. Not living in the inner courtyard like Penny, Cathy and Dickie, I had no internal access to the house. So, buttoning my coat up to my chin, and pulling my cap over my eyes, I dashed through the sleet and past the swaying tree on my toes, trying not to spoil my shoes. The door echoed with a hollow thud as I entered the back of the house and hung up my coat and cap in the gloom. There is never much light in the Abbey corridors; despite the availability of energy-saving light bulbs, the frugal habits of a lifetime die hard. The panelling creaked in the draughts, and my footsteps sounded lightly on the stone-flagged floor as I passed the darker patches of shadow that indicated corridors leading to the tack room (now long given over to cuttings, croquet sets and cats), conservatory, and kitchen, respectively. At last, crossing the dining room, I heard the muffled sound of voices, and entering the library was welcomed by the light and warmth of a roaring fire.

It was lovely to see so many of the family gathered together for Christmas. William was back from his travels, and there were his two sons, and daughters-in-law, and all the grandchildren.

As I took my glass from Helena she looked down at Theophrastes and said rather frostily, 'Well, you *are* making yourself at home, aren't you?'

I smiled ruefully, and gravitated towards the fire. 'Goodness; what was that all about?' said Cathy as we approached.

'I'm afraid that Theophrastes and I are in the cat-house just at the moment', I said.

'Good heavens, why?'

'You obviously haven't heard the joyous news;' I said. 'Cleopatra has just had a litter of kittens. Unfortunately they are odd-looking, mottled little creatures, with small heads and big ears, and long legs and tails. I fear that DNA testing will not be necessary to establish paternity.'

'You don't mean to say —' she broke off, looking at Theophrastes with a twinkle in her eye. 'But I thought they didn't *like* each other.'

'I'm not sure that cats care much about liking. That might just have made it a greater challenge.' Theophrastes, typically, had insinuated himself close to the fire, and sat licking a paw. 'And there's no point in you sitting there looking oriental and inscrutable,' I added, catching the culprit's disdainful eye. He turned his head in profile and gave a dismissive flick of his tail. 'We have since paid a visit to the vet,' I continued to Cathy, 'but it is rather a case of shutting the cat flap after the tom has got out'.

At this point Penny appeared beside us through a door in the panelling. She had obviously taken the circuitous internal route from her apartment to the library, rather than braving the elements. 'Good evening, good evening,' she said, passing us to go and pay her compliments to the family. As my eyes returned to the fireplace I was suddenly aware of a huge blank space where the painting over the mantel should have been.

'Good heavens!' I said; 'What's happened to the first Earl?'

'He's away being cleaned,' answered Helena, coming up to us. 'It was Mark's idea. It's the sort of thing one never gets round to, like cleaning curtains. I wasn't sure of the expense, but Mark has arranged it through his contacts, and it isn't that bad at all. The paintings have been going two at a time, and I have to say that they look a lot better for cleaning. I had no idea how colourful some of them were! This one ought to come out particularly well; as far as I know it has been hanging over that fireplace since it was painted.'

There was a sudden gust of wind, and the lights faltered for a moment, leaving us in the glow of fire and candle light. 'I was sure there would be blackouts over the holidays,' continued Helena with resignation. 'I've put candles all over the place. It's always during a holiday, when there's no chance of getting things repaired for days. I hope that Dickie and Mark make it over without being plunged into darkness; we can sort everyone out with torches if necessary for going back.'

'I didn't actually see any signs of life from the other apartments on my way over here. Are you sure that Dickie is coming this evening?' I said.

'Isn't he in Indonesia having his new teeth put in?' said Cathy.

'Oh, is that what he's going for? He was rather coy about explanations; and one doesn't like to ask, in case it's business, as it so often is with him. But, no, I gather that trip is for later in the new year.'

'Oh,' said Cathy; 'that's irritating. I was surprised not to see him yesterday for dinner. He usually comes. Perhaps he's away somewhere else.'

'Oh I don't think so; at any rate he did say he'd be here this evening.'

'When were you speaking to him?' I asked.

'Just last week, wasn't it Will,' she said, turning to her husband, who concurred. 'Yes, I remember because it was just before the concert, and I was going into Rathcoole for my last thrash through the supermarkets. He said he would be here for the holidays, and off again towards the end of January.'

There was a spatter of hail on the window, and conversation failed. At last Cathy grasped the nettle and said, 'When exactly did anyone see Dickie last? Has anyone seen him since the concert?' There was silence.

'I usually do a bit of shopping for him when he's about,' said Penny. 'You know, when I'm up in Greenborough doing my own, I get a few things for him. Especially if shops are going to be closed for a holiday. Always, Christmas and Easter, he pops a little list through my door before the last shopping day. But he didn't this year.'

'Now you know, that really is rather odd,' said William. 'I do hope that he's well; it would be dreadful to think of him ill in his apartment, and not able to contact anyone. The west tower is rather remote.'

'He's got his phone . . .' said Cathy, doubtfully. There was a thoughtful silence.

'When he didn't come to you for dinner yesterday, Cathy,' Penny continued, 'I assumed that he had told you that he would be away. Not that I've ever known him to be away at Christmas. Where would he go? But if he's staying here over the holidays, what is he eating?'

'Do you know,' said William at last, 'I think I'd be happier just to check up and make sure he's alright.'

'I knocked on his door coming down tonight, but got no reply,' continued Penny.

'But his car was definitely there as I came across,' I said; 'in fact, I'm sure it's been there for at least a week. Though he does sometimes take a taxi into Rathcoole if he's going to be away for awhile.'

'I'll go,' said the Chancellors' younger son George, picking up a candelabrum and moving towards the door that Penny had come in through. But for some reason, William followed after him, and then Cathy, and then the children, and Theophrastes. And so somehow we all found ourselves filing through the dark staircases and corridors behind the flames of the candles, with a growing sense of foreboding. The panelling and stairs creaked in the dark, and the thin whistling of draughts circulated from unseen sources. At last we arrived at the west tower apartment, and stood gathered in front of the door. William knocked. There was silence. He knocked louder. Still no sound. He called. No reply. He called louder. Nothing.

'Shall I check?' asked George. At a nod from William, he tried the door, and found that it was unlocked. After knocking again, he went in. As we watched from the doorway, he turned on the light of the sitting room and set the candelabrum on Dickie's desk. Gradually we all came in, and stood inside the door while George and William looked through the flat. 'No one,' William said, reappearing from the bedroom. We began to breathe again. But as George went to lift the candelabrum he said, 'That's odd,' and we stiffened. 'His passport is here, and his phone, and cheque-book, and the keys of his car, just as if he were planning to go off somewhere.'

'And his overcoat is behind the door,' said Cathy. 'And his hat and scarf.'

'Well,' said Helena sensibly, 'that simply means that he's about the house somewhere. So we'd better go back to the library before he finds us here poking among his socks.'

'Speaking of socks,' said William, 'there is a set of clothes in the bedroom, neatly folded on a chair, and a pair of shoes beneath. There's also a small suitcase on the bed, half-packed.'

'Well, there you are then,' said Helena. 'That must be in preparation for his trip, like his passport and so on. He's obviously changed for the evening, and has already gone to the library. He's probably there now, eating all the sausage rolls.' At this there was a panicked agitation among the children.

'But *how*?' said Penny. 'He can hardly have passed us; and the only other way down would be to go out into the courtyard and come in by the back door. But why would he do that? He would hardly change for the evening and then go for a stroll in this weather. He was supposed to come to sherry this evening. And he didn't come to Christmas dinner yesterday. He hasn't any shopping in,' she continued, going into the kitchenette and opening the refrigerator. 'No, he hasn't. And the milk has gone off,' she said, sniffing the carton. And he can't have gone out in his car. So *where is he*?'

At this point George returned to the bedroom, and coming out said, 'His evening clothes are there, and his favourite sports jacket and brogues. His pyjamas are under the pillow, his dressing gown is behind the door, and his slippers are under the bed.' The wind hissed at the windows and whistled round the castellations outside as we stood silently, unable to think of any benign answer to this puzzle. Then gradually, softly, but growing inexorably louder, came another sound on the wind.

'*What's that*?' cried Penny, as George's faltering hand put the candelabrum back on the desk. I could literally feel the hair rise on my head, as the strains of a low, vibrating melody echoed through the stone of the walls.

'It can only be . . .' began William.

'*But that's impossible*!' said Helena, visibly shaken, as the strains of an organ rose through the rain. 'It hasn't played for two hundred years!'

And suddenly we were all hurtling headlong down corridors and stairways back towards the library. I don't know that anyone even paused to turn out the lights or close the door of Dickie's apartment. At one point I fell behind the others, and was on the point of taking a wrong turning towards the east wing, when a stern hiss from Theophrastes brought me right, and I followed him to the library. The others had already passed through it to the Great Hall. The sound of the organ was deafening now, swelling into the vault of the Hall with the full force of its pipes. Hurtling into the room I all but collided with the others, as they stood frozen to the spot, watching Mark Charles letting out all the stops and obviously enjoying his performance. At length he stopped, and turned round to us with a smile, doubtless expecting the applause that his playing deserved. But the smile died on his lips as he saw our pale, shocked expressions. He began to suspect that he had committed some dreadful *faux pas*.

'I'm so sorry,' he began; 'I hope that it was alright for me to play. Last time I tried the organ it didn't work at all. I haven't done it any harm, honestly,' he continued, gently closing the cover over the keys. 'When I came into the library no one was there, and I thought that I must have got the day wrong. But there were lots of glasses and things, so I decided that you must all have wandered off somewhere else for a while, and I thought I'd potter about a bit until you came back. I say; is everything alright?'

At this point there was a torrent of hail and sleet, and the lights went out for good. We stood spellbound in the light of the candelabrum until Cathy said, 'Do you know, I think I need a sherry.'

'Well I don't know about the rest of you, but I need a brandy, at least,' said Helena. 'Poor Mark, do come out of this cold while we get you a mince pie. Let's all have a drink while we decide whether we ought to call the Guards.'

'Why whatever is going on?' asked Mark, realising that something was seriously amiss.

'Come in to the fire, and we'll explain', I said.

'And I think it's time for the children to be in bed,' said William, to which the usual protests were made, as you may well imagine. But they were finally bundled off to the nursery by their mothers with a plate of sausage rolls and mince pies, and the promise of being allowed to watch *Nightmare on Elm Street*. Heaven knows, they were probably better equipped to deal with disappearing tenants and haunted organs than we were!

THE SERPENT IN THE GARDEN

It will come as no surprise that it was concluded that the Guards did need to be informed. It will equally come as no surprise that they said that they would give Dickie a couple of days to turn up. I dare say they thought that he was wandering about in the slush in his underwear, starving; and as they would see it, probably under the influence of drink as well. It was William who removed himself discreetly with a candle and made all the necessary telephone calls — to the Guards, and to any of Dickie's friends who might conceivably know where he was. Helena filled glasses and threw a log on the fire as we explained the circumstances to Mark (making as light as we could, I might say, of our alarms.) Somehow the normality of finding him at the organ had brought us to our senses. Yes, Dickie seemed to have disappeared under suspicious circumstances. But it was being reported to the Guards, and that was all that we could do. It wasn't as if we had found evidence of a crime. As Penny passed round the sausage rolls and mince pies we discovered that they were still warm; and indeed, it must only have been a quarter of an hour or so ago that we had first gone to check on Dickie's flat. As the fire blazed up afresh and the drinks warmed our blood, a relaxed and friendly atmosphere developed, that we wouldn't have thought possible a mere few minutes before. We speculated on what sort of holiday Claudia would be having with her family. 'I assume that you'll be going out to spend the New Year with her, Mark. Will you be coming back together?' asked Helena as she stirred the fire.

J.E. RUTHERFORD

The poor fellow blushed and started. 'Why, yes, as a matter of fact. I've been invited to be part of the twinning committee, and . . .'

'Oh, yes, quite, all that too . . .' said Helena enigmatically, moving back to the drinks tray.

'*How does she do that*?' Mark asked, of no one in particular.

'No one knows,' said Cathy. 'You get used to it eventually.'

In the flickering shadows, no one felt like leaving the warmth of the fire and the company to return in darkness and alone to their own apartment. But at length there was no longer any excuse to prolong the party. When William returned and reported the conversations he had had, it marked a natural end to the evening. George and Mark returned to Dickie's flat, checked it once again, and, finding the key, locked it. By this time Penny was asleep on a settee, and Cathy and I were feeling the exhaustion that follows a prolonged shock. Gratefully accepting a torch, we gently roused Penny, and the four of us set off together for our own beds. Mark and I escorted Penny and Cathy to their apartments, through the interior of the Abbey. Once we had made sure that they had their candles and fires lit, and had settled them in for the night (with instructions to lock their doors), we turned our collars against the rain and dashed across the courtyard to our respective apartments. Theophrastes had prevented me long since, and I found him curled in a lump under the bedclothes at the bottom of my bed.

11
Ghosts on the Bog

The weeks went by, the days lengthened, and there was still no sign of Dickie. He was officially listed as a missing person, though to some of us it seemed easier, and less sinister, to think that he had done a runner, for reasons as yet unclear. Mr Moto returned with the swallows, so to speak, and treated us to a presentation one evening of his videos of cairns, passage tombs, and solar alignments. It was rather embarrassing to find how much more of our own heritage he understood than we did. True to Helena's intuition, Claudia reappeared after the holidays together with Mark Charles, and it was now evident that they had become an item. I had been bemused, coming into the winter, as to what could be keeping Claudia in Ireland once the newts began their hibernation; her assertions that she was compiling statistics only begged the question of how much data there could be to compile. A spreadsheet for every newt?

But now, she and Mark were both members of the Ardliss twinning committee, which was preparing to make an official tie between us and Claudia's village, Santa Maria degli Angeli. I must say that the prospect did much to cheer us all in the freezing depths of February; we hoped very much that there would be reciprocal visits between the two towns, and that they wouldn't be restricted to members of the respective twinning committees. The entrepreneurs among us were hoping to find new markets for our excellent local beef, lamb and honey. Helena was already putting feelers out about the possibility of marketing her new variety of wheat in Italy, since Angela had informed her that Italian wheat tends not to be as hard as that produced on the plains of places such as North America. By contrast, the greedy among us (which I confess included myself, as well as, of course, Angela Carrington and Fr Enda), were eager for the imports that were likely to travel in the opposite direction.

Only the Avakians were less than enthusiastic, when they returned to find that the twinning plan was firmly settled. At a public meeting on the project, held in the Community Centre, Cosmas explained that he and Maria had very much hoped that something similar might have been arranged with a town in one of the eastern European countries from which so many of our new neighbours originate. There was a genuine and widespread regret at the meeting that it wouldn't be possible to enter into two such projects at the same time. But it was agreed that less formal ties should be established with some of the other, new EU member states, whose citizens were settling among us. There was particular enthusiasm for the idea of inviting some of our local newcomers to give us talks on their own towns and cities of origin, and to explain a little about their motives for moving to Ireland. The Avakians accepted the sense of this, and I think came to realise that this was a more reasonable first step than jumping into a twinning project straight away. And so it was that the whole idea of our new ties to Italy became a greatly anticipated treat, and Angela found herself in demand for Italian conversation lessons and cookery demonstrations.

As to the mystery of the playing organ, Helena had put a firm veto on any attempt to resolve it. 'If anyone tries so much as to open the case,' she had said, 'the whole thing is bound to fall into pieces. I haven't the least interest in why it has started to work; perhaps something is nesting in it.'

'If so, it's deaf by now, if not paralysed with fright,' observed Penny.

'Well, that can't be helped at this stage,' continued Helena. 'But I intend to make hay (or in this case music), while the sun shines, without looking a gift horse in the mouth, to mix metaphors.'

At first Helena only allowed Mark Charles and the respective parish organists limited access to the instrument, for fear of breaking the spell. But they all three assured her that there were no signs of it packing in. And so gradually the Abbey filled with music, and it was decided that the first public performance on the newly resuscitated Abbey organ would be held in the summer, as part of the twinning festivities. 'But I'll have a couple of harpists on stand-by, just in case the organ implodes again first,' she said, unwilling to believe that the luck would hold.

And so the dreary February days passed slowly towards March, lightened only by the prospect of Italian sunshine to come (if only vicariously) in the summer, and the swelling strains of the organ. I found the days drag particularly since I was without the companionship of Cathy. She had finally been called in to hospital to be given her new knee; and although these days this sort of surgery requires only a short stay as an in-patient, the convalescent and rehabilitation processes still take time. She had therefore gone to her son's family to recuperate. 'Though how,' I put it to her, 'you are to rest in the midst of all those children, horses and dogs is a mystery to me! You'd be better off here where we could look after you.' But it is of course always a comfort to be in the bosom of one's own family at such times. Cathy's daughter-in-law is a trained nurse, so she could hardly have been in better hands. From my own, selfish point of view, however, it was inconvenient, to say the least. I had a small, ancient sports car, which I didn't trust out in bad weather. I was therefore limited in February and March to what shopping I was able to do locally on the scooter. And although I have no criticism of the produce available in Ardliss, scooters are not best suited to winter use, however circumscribed the distances travelled. I had grown used to sharing a lift with Cathy in her little Fiat *Seicento* for shopping in Rathcoole during the worst of the winter months, and I now realised how much I had come to take that for granted. And so it was that the only thing I had to relieve the tedium of the season was anticipating the twinning, and editing the proofs of my new book on Pythagorean themes in the early Greek fathers of the Church.

For others, though, the winter seemed to pass pleasantly enough. Within a short time, Claudia Crespi had given up even pretending to think about newts. One used to come upon her with Mark, walking hand in hand with him down the pond path, and doubtless enthusing about all the wonderful things that would shortly be emerging, hatching, and sprouting there. Even devoted nature lovers find this sort of thing difficult to get excited about in February. But such is the power of love to fire the imagination, that Mark always looked enraptured as he walked arm in arm with Claudia, both of them bundled up in wellies and coats and fluffy hats, looking like a pair of teddy bears in search of a picnic. For Mark's part, he was able to reciprocate in a rather more comfortable fashion by talking to Claudia indoors about art and furniture. We tend to assume that all Italians are passionate about art, but the truth is, as Angela Carrington always reminds us, that what they are really passionate about is *la dolce vita*. Food, clothes, friends and music are far more essential components of Italian life than paintings — though these and sculpture form part of that backdrop to their daily dramas that Italians tend to take for granted. And so Claudia didn't appear to be at all resentful of Mark's superior knowledge of these things. And they could hardly have had a more useful context for pursuing their conversations. They were constantly to be found about the Abbey, gazing at a portrait, or discussing a table. Indeed, we became so used to bumping into them when we turned corners or entered a room that I began to feel that they had been invested with the ghost of Michael Slattery. It was a relief, to me at least, when they became friendly with Debbie English and began haunting her studio instead.

Given my confinement to the area immediately around Ardliss, it was awhile before I became acquainted with news of the dramas (or melodramas) occurring at the other end of our parish, up towards Noyestown. And I am not referring here to the rumours of the water sports centre to be built on Lough Coile. While not wishing to be uncharitable, I'm afraid that we had our field by the school to worry about, and it was up to them to worry about their lake. No, the news from up along the bog road was far more enigmatic and puzzling. The vehicle that the Carringtons had seen on the bog on their way home from the Lynnes' on Christmas Eve had now become, as is the inexorable fate of unexplained sights, a ghostly apparition. It was said that it was a ghost hearse, searching for the souls of the unbaptised who had been interred in the bog centuries ago. This sort of rumour would ordinarily have suffered the fate of all such winter fireside tales, had it not been for the fact that 'ghosts' had persisted in reappearing on the bog road into February. The hearse, it seemed, had shot off the bog one foggy night, passing before a startled motorist and then proceeding before him noiselessly up the Noyestown road before suddenly darting back onto the bog. The carriage was said to be pulled by four black horses, the whole equipage moving along at a height of some four feet above the ground.

And then other nocturnal phenomena began to be observed on the bog, particularly along that same stretch of road going up towards Noyestown. Flickering torches were seen hovering about in the mist, and then fairy lights, entrancing the unwary and leading them on into the bog until they were lured into treacherous patches of mud, and then disappearing. It seemed incredible to me that anyone would get out of their car on a foggy night and follow lights onto the bog, but that apparently was what Matthew Carrington had done, coming home one January evening after calling on Wendy Noyes in the Lough Coile nursing home, where she was staying for a temporary rest. Although it was not yet six o'clock, it was dark, with drifts of fog. He had been growing increasingly impatient with the ghostly rumours, and he tended to blame himself for having started them in the first place. And so when he again saw the dark shape of a vehicle on the bog, and a flickering light, he pulled up his car, and taking a torch set out to find out what exactly was going on.

As everyone who has ever done such a thing on a foggy night will know, it is not long before one's bearings become confused. Matthew found himself looking around frequently to steer himself with reference to the position of his car, but its outline grew fainter as he progressed onto the bog. And when there was a billow of fog on the road it disappeared altogether, sometimes for a matter of a couple of minutes at a time. Being too sensible to become lost on a bog at night, he had decided to turn back once he could see the car clearly again. Then, turning his eyes back to the bog one last time, there was a wafted clearing in the mist, and he found himself confronting a small, black figure not ten feet in front of him. He gasped despite himself, and was still in the process of steadying his nerves when another billow of fog obscured the figure. When it cleared the figure was of course gone, and all that was visible where it had been was a stunted thorn bush. Genuinely shaken, Matthew had made his way back to his car, and sat there several minutes before nerving himself to continue his drive home.

After he had related his adventure to Angela, he remained uncertain what to do. He was loth to add fuel to what he still considered to be irrational rumours. On the other hand he could not bring himself to believe that he had been mistaken in what he had seen. Despite the gloomy atmosphere and bad weather, he was convinced of the solidity of the figure. He tried to fix its appearance in his mind, in case he should have occasion to need to describe it. As far as he could define it, it was a featureless black figure, about the size of a gnome (meaning a gnome of legend, rather than the garden variety). He knew that, were he to let this become generally known, it would fuel the rumours with the added interest value of fairies and little people.

And so it was several weeks before I, or anyone in Ardliss, began to hear of the incident. It was after church and over coffee one Sunday that I overheard Matthew's conversation with the glebe warden, Arthur. Arthur works up towards Noyestown, and travels along the bog roads daily; and he is moreover a sensible sort of fellow.

THE SERPENT IN THE GARDEN

So it was perhaps inevitable that sooner or later Matthew would discuss the mystery with him.

'Have you heard about Matthew's fright?' asked Bea Turner, having observed me listening in on his conversation with Arthur.

'I've only just been overhearing something of it just now,' I said. 'What's it all about?'

Bea filled me in on the details. As Matthew's Lay Pastoral Assistant, and distributor of newsletters, she was of course fully informed. Bea and Frank, however, live out between the Greenborough and Dublin roads, and their geography could hardly be more different to that of the bog. Once the land rises to the north and east of the bog, it immediately turns into steep hills and innumerable little lakes, culminating in a high ridge on the edge of a plain. This ridge is marked by cairns and megalithic passage tombs. The Turners' house is nestled in the hills between the bog and the plain, on the side of a hill, and overlooking a pretty little hidden lake.

'What do you make of it?' I asked her when she had finished telling me the story.

'I can't make anything out of it at all, nor I'm sure can anyone else; though of course that won't stop people trying. It really is curious; Matthew isn't at all given to nerves or wild imagination, yet he is quite certain about what he saw.'

'Well,' I said, 'I would advise him to suppress that bit about the thorn bush; we all know where *that* will lead.'

'I know; that really is odd. It's the sort of thing you would expect more up our way, up by the cairns.'

'I must mention some of those old legends to Mr Moto,' I said. 'I wonder whether he's interested in folk traditions? Given his love of all things megalithic and Celtic, I daresay he would be enthralled by that sort of thing, if he doesn't already know more about it than we do. You must come across him quite a bit out your way, hunting for stone age remains.'

'Not so much these days,' she said. 'In the summer and autumn we used to see a lot of him up on the cairns, but I don't think I've seen him since the Solstice. After Newgrange our tombs must seem pretty small beer. He's probably found something new to move on to now.'

'So it seems; he's begun to enthuse about knights again,' I said. 'I believe that he's planning to move on to the Continent some time this summer. We'll probably start getting postcards from Köln and Carcassonne. I wonder whether he'll take up an interest in Cathars and Albigensians? Whatever he gets on to I hope he'll come back to give us another of his presentations. He really is quite depressingly well informed. It must be lovely to have the means to lead such an ideal life for a *dilettante* scholar.'

And so it was that the mystery of the black gnome seemed likely to fade in our collective memory in much the same way that Dickie's disappearance had. There had of course been no shortage of people to suggest that the gnome was in fact Dickie's restless ghost, and that his body was buried somewhere on the bog. The fact that the apparitions had begun about the time that Dickie had disappeared was not lost on anyone. Though why a substantial, healthy man of six feet should produce a gnome-sized ghost was something no one cared to explain. But as I say, just when these mysteries might have been expected to lose their prominence in our minds, the first tangible evidence came to light of something rum happening on the bog.

This time it was Bob Macnamee, the builder. Coming down through the bog from Noyestown one evening, he was keeping an eye out for suspicious lights etc. when he saw the dark shape of the 'hearse' out on the bog. But Bob, unlike Matthew Carrington, is a native of Greenborough, and a housing developer besides; he is reasonably well acquainted with the main tracks across the bog, and suspected that the thing he saw was on one. The evening was, in addition, clear, so when he saw the fairy light, he turned of the road on to a track, and made as best he could in the direction of the apparition. But the track ran out, or else he had taken a wrong turning. He could drive no further, and got out to pursue on foot. He could still glimpse the light intermittently, though the shape of the vehicle was now lost in the formless shadows that the moonlight cast among the bog trees. At length, straining forward to catch a glimpse of the light again, he caught his foot on a root and fell heavily; he was winded, and had bruised his head. He therefore sat a moment before cursing himself for a fool and deciding to head back as best he could to his vehicle. But as he stood and brushed himself off, he saw, a matter of only a dozen yards or so ahead, a large black blob. Thinking that he might as well see what it was before returning, he circled round it to the side best lit by the moon. Suddenly, a cloud obscured the moonlight, and all he was left seeing in front of him was the sickly, luminous glow of a grinning face.

There is no need for me to describe, or indeed for you to speculate upon, the effect that this had on him. Turning, he tore through the scrub and fell through the peat cuttings until he had located his lorry. Speedily regaining the road, instead of carrying on to Ardliss he returned as quickly as he could to Noyestown, where he raised the alarm. There was of course nothing to be done at that time of night, and so at length he headed home, this time via Greenborough. But he had arranged that on the following day he would meet some of the farmers who live around the bog, and take them as nearly as he could to the spot where he had seen the face. After much searching and cogitating they duly found the marks left by Bob's lorry where it had lost the track. Following, as well as they were able, his recollection of his movements, they at length saw something black flapping in the wind. Of hearse, gnome, or black blob there was no trace. Only the shredded remains of a silage bag caught in a tree, where it had evidently blown. There was nothing else. So, for want of anything else to do, they went over to the tree to look at the silage bag. And there, as they untwisted it to examine it, they found a round, white smiley face.

12
Spring at Blandings

It is difficult to describe to those who aren't familiar with it, the exhilaration of mounting a horse for the first time after a long period of deprivation. I had spent the best part of a year having my upper back and shoulder treated by a chiropractor following a bad fall. But now here I was, as the first buds appeared in the growing warmth of a March sun, sniffing the crisp, clean air from a long-familiar perspective, as Tricksy Mouse moved restlessly beneath me. Rising five, she could be expected to have reached the age of discretion, and Stevie had selected her as suitable for my first ride out. 'She shouldn't give you any surprises,' he said as he sidled up on someone I hadn't met before, adjusting his chin strap. Alice appeared, walking across the yard, and Steve called out, 'Aren't you ready yet?'

'Can I ride Grouse Mouse?' she asked (there being a colony of Mice in the yard just then, progeny of the great Mouseketeer).

'You certainly cannot! No one touches her except Tony, especially right now.'

'But I can ride as well as Robbie,' she persisted, and I sensed that this was the continuation of an earlier conversation. I suspected that Alice would have preferred Tricksy to her own retired gelding.

'Alice!'

'Well, I can.'

'I'm sure you can!' I intervened before Steve could reply. 'The thing to remember is that the older you get, the harder the ground becomes. I'm sure that your father gave me Tricksy out of consideration for my bones.'

'Would you go get Dirty Flirty, or we'll leave you behind. You were wild to have him when he came off the track, and I don't know why I bought him for you if you don't like him anymore.'

'Oh, all right,' she said with resignation, entering a box stall and returning with Flirty already saddled and ready to go. He was really a very handsome gelding, and was turning into a useful hunter. But Alice longed for a jockey's license, and this was an ongoing source of tension between her and her father.

Alice got up, and the three of us set off down the lane that would bring us eventually past the back gate of Blandings, and so on through the dairy farm and at last to the large open expanse that had, from time immemorial, been known as the Galloping Green. It was to be a nice, gentle outing to start getting me fit again. It was also a welcome opportunity to have a good chat with Steve. Over the past year I had come to realise that I only really got a chance to talk to him on horseback. He was always so busy with the yard, and he didn't really have hobbies to speak of.

'It seems like an age since we've talked,' I said.

'I know; time has been getting away from me,' he replied. 'It seems only a few weeks ago that the Guards were swarming around because of that idiot Slattery, and now we look like having it all over again with Dickie. I have to say that I'll be sad if anything has happened to him. Do you remember when he and Cathy seemed so grown up to us? When they used to judge the Pony Club gymkhana I was so envious; I wanted to be as grown up as Dickie, and have a moustache just like his. Looking back at it, he must only have been about twenty at the time, but even then he carried himself like a man of the world.'

'Yes; he was a real favourite with all the girls, too' I said. 'He was the nearest thing in the midlands to a film star. Poor Dickie. You know, I have a bad feeling about his disappearance. Even though I can't think of anything that could have put his life in danger, I simply can't believe that there is going to turn out to be a harmless explanation for this. And yet I never knew him to do worse than speculate in business and property. Of course that doesn't prove anything; I was hardly in his confidence. It's just that I would be surprised to find that he was really involved in something very criminal. Unlike Michael Slattery. I confidently expect, in the fulness of time, to discover that he was mixed up with real criminals. And whatever it was, perhaps Dickie found out about it.'

'If he did, he should have gone to the Guards,' observed Steve. 'But I think that that was one of his fatal flaws — well, not *fatal*, I hope — but he always played a lone hand. And that's a guaranteed way to come unstuck sooner or later. And I'm afraid that I don't agree with you about Slattery. He was a silly, mountebank little fellow. Always surrounding himself with airs of mystery.

144

No real criminal wants to draw that much attention to himself.'

'Are you very sure that he wasn't involved in any illegal betting?' I ventured tentatively. 'There seems to be a prevailing opinion that he was doing that, or even that he was mixed up in race fixing.'

At this Steve just laughed. 'You see? That's exactly what I mean. He's managed to make a big reputation for himself as a track wheeler-dealer, when he wasn't anything at all. No one who was mixed up in serious racing fraud would cultivate such a suspicious manner. They wouldn't last five minutes. Michael Slattery would have liked everyone to think that he was some big time conman, but I've never heard any evidence that he did anything illegal at all. I don't think there was actually any harm in him; I just got tired of his act. He wasn't up to making his own book; he just took bets to the races for people, and tried to make a mystery about it.'

'But you always seemed so hostile about him,' I said, taking my courage in my hands.

Steve sighed. 'That's because his confounded mystery always ended up enveloping other people around him. People with reputations, who can't afford melodrama or question marks. Take that thing about people saying I was up to something. It's silly, and I can bear any amount of investigation. But it's nasty for people even to think that sort of thing about you, and it's bound to leave a mark on your name, however innocent you are. People always have a sneaking suspicion that there's no smoke without fire. I really had no patience with his games, because he didn't know how seriously they could be taken.'

We continued along in silence until we reached the gallop, and then our attention returned to the business at hand. But as I collected up my scooter from the yard to return home at the end of the morning, I couldn't help wondering if this would indeed turn out to account for Michael's murder. Had his air of mystery compromised the safety of someone who really was as dangerous as Michael pretended to be?

Once I had showered and put on clean clothes, I was aware that my muscles were going to complain about the unaccustomed exercise. So I decided to take a walk to cool down slowly, and hopefully stave off the worst aches and pains. But on my way through the courtyard I encountered Helena struggling with a box of books.

'Oh, thank heavens, Robbie; could you just help me with these?'

I grasped one side of the box to share the load. 'Where are they going?' I asked.

'Back to the chapel. The bindings have been restored.'

'What are they?' I asked again.

'Very ancient Books of Common Prayer. Quite useless now. They've been sitting in the chapel forever. We would probably have thrown them out sooner or later; they're not legal any more of course, and in any case the chapel is only really used for weddings and

Christenings nowadays. But Mark said that they were valuable, so we got the bindings repaired. We still don't need them in the chapel, of course, but I'm just putting them in there in the meantime until we decide whether to sell them.'

We had reached the chapel door, and I balanced the box against the wall while Helena opened it and found the light. 'I didn't know that Mark was an authority on old books as well as furniture,' I said.

'I don't think he is, really,' said Helena as we carefully set the box on a table at the back of the chapel. 'I think he just likes old things generally. Furniture of course is his field of expertise, but he knows a fair bit about paintings and books and that sort of thing, too.'

'I must invite him in to see my library,' I said; 'I have some curious tomes he might like to see.'

'I'm sure he would like that,' said Helena, resting her weight against the end of one of the stalls that run along the sides of the chapel. 'Oh dear!' she then exclaimed, turning to the panel she was leaning against and shaking it. 'Oh good, I think it's just loose,' she said, examining it more closely. 'No sign of rot or beetles, thankfully.

'Did you hear about our panic over death-watch beetle?' she asked as we moved to leave the chapel.

'No, indeed!' I said. 'You don't mean to say there is some? It will be a terribly big job to cure if there is.'

'No one knows that better than I,' Helena replied. 'I used to stay with cousins sometimes in a house that was in a continual state of being eaten and restored. I tend to be rather sensitive about the subject. That's how our latest scare came about. I had stayed up late to finish reading something,' she continued as she locked the chapel door, 'so it was late when I came to bed and put out the light. I was just lying there, thinking about the book I had been reading, when I heard the dreaded 'tock' coming from the ceiling above. It had been a long day, and I really wasn't in the mood for yet another crisis, so I'm afraid I put earplugs in and just went to sleep. But of course the next morning the thing had to be confronted. I have a reasonable grasp of what to look for, so before calling anyone in I got up into the roof space. And do you know what I found? A little electronic toy, making periodic 'tock' sounds. Well, of course it was a relief, but I confess that it irritated me.'

'And who turned out to be responsible?' I asked, smiling.

'Oh, it had to be Rupert. He was the only grandchild here this weekend. He recognised it at once. Apparently Mr Moto brought several back with him, and has given them to all the children. And do you know, after scolding him for giving me a fright, all he had to say was, "I hope it hasn't died". I said it obviously hadn't, because it was making a noise and the display was still showing. But he said that wasn't what he meant. It might have died of starvation or thirst. At this point I began to worry about him, but he explained that the thing is actually a 'virtual pet'; if you don't feed it and water it and take it for walks, it dies. I must say that it sounds like a good idea for a toy; children are always forgetting to look after their pets. I asked Rupert why it went 'tock', and he was very relieved that it did. Apparently that's what it does when it wants food or water. At any rate, that was the end of the crisis. Though I can't imagine how Rupert got up into the roof space. But then children always do get everywhere.'

By now it was nearly one o'clock, so I decided to postpone my walk until after lunch. I had a nice piece of salmon fillet, and as I entered my kitchen I found Theophrastes waiting impatiently. If he had had a watch, he would have been pointing at it accusingly. Anyone would have thought that I had bought the fillet just for him!

After lunch I looked out the window and saw that the afternoon was as lovely as the morning had been. I decided to take my walk up to the old stable, to see Debbie. I realised as I set out that I hadn't been there since the day that Michael's murder weapon had been found. It was in riding past that morning that it had occurred to me to pay Debbie a visit, but now, recollecting that last occasion, I thought to return first to my kitchen and collect a few cuttings I had growing on the window sill. I put them in an old game bag, and slung it over my shoulder. It had been a while since I had last seen Sinead, and it would be nice to call and leave her some *dianthus* for summer planting.

Luck was with me, and she was at home, in the midst of boys and spaniels. I thought that she looked very well, and just like her old self. I had a cup of tea with her, and chatted about the shop and the children, and gave her the cuttings. It had cheered me considerably to find them all so well, so as I turned in at the stable yard gate it was with difficulty that I recalled the atmosphere that had surrounded my last visit there. As I was about to knock at the door of the studio, it opened in front of me and there was Claudia, looking back inside and saying, 'It won't be too difficult, will it?'

To which Debbie's voice replied from inside, 'No; it's the original that's difficult, not copies.'

Claudia then turned to go and jumped as she saw me, looking disconcerted.

'I'm so sorry to have startled you,' I said; 'I've just come to call on Debbie and hear how her work is progressing.'

'Oh, yes, of course; I am just leaving,' Claudia said; and, bidding a quick goodbye to Debbie, she rushed off.

As I entered the studio, Debbie was just throwing a sheet over something. She had of course heard my conversation with Claudia, and as she turned to me she said, 'Claudia is helping me with a figure I'm doing. But I'm afraid that it's rather a secret, so I'd appreciate it if you didn't mention it to anyone.'

'Certainly not,' I said; 'I'm sorry to barge in while you're busy. I always seem to interrupt your work when I call, and that's something that I find irritating myself.'

'No, no; we'd finished for today. Would you like a cup of tea?'

'I've just had one with Sinead, thanks; I just thought I'd look in while I was out this way.'

'I'm having a break now anyway, honestly. I'm putting the kettle on for myself, so feel free to join me if you'd like,' she said warmly.

So I acquiesced, and we were soon sitting in the southern sun that shone through her kitchen window. 'The studio looks a lot tidier than when I last saw it,' I said.

'Oh, yes!' Debbie answered cheerfully. 'Gosh, that seems a long time ago, when you were last here.'

'Well, I suppose it was, really, especially in terms of your working year. I can't imagine how you manage to teach and still do your own work. I found it nearly impossible when I was lecturing full-time. I'm extremely lucky to have my readership,' I said.

I don't teach full time any more,' Debbie said, 'and from next year I'm thinking of resigning altogether.'

'Are you very sure?' I asked, taken aback. 'Teaching jobs are so hard to come by; it will be hard to get another if you change your mind.'

'Yes, I know. And I worked hard to get this one. But I've made more this year in commissions than teaching; and what I earn as an artist is tax free, but not what I earn teaching. I'm about to enter a very serious competition in New York, and if I do at all well in that, it should put my name on the map.'

'All the same,' I said, 'a salary, however humble, is something to count on. On the other hand, I can well see that for an artist, creative work is more rewarding than teaching.'

'Oh, it doesn't have to be,' Debbie said. 'But for teaching to be really rewarding, you have to have gifted, motivated students. It's the same for me as for you, or for anyone. If I managed to make a name for myself, I would want students in my studio. There's nothing like other artists to stimulate your imagination and stretch you technically.'

'I didn't realise that there was still any studio tradition these days in the visual arts,' I said. 'I'm glad to learn that there is.'

'Oh, there still is, but it's hard to get into a first-rate studio, and even harder to set up on your own with students who are any good. That would have to be a long-term aspiration for me. There will be a lot of long, hard grind in the meantime, and I have to take it one step at a time. But if I do well in this competition I'll be in a strong enough position to take a break from teaching at least, and still be able to find a job again if I decide I want to.'

I was extremely pleased to learn that Debbie's career had taken off so very well. There were indeed very few things in her studio just then. I obviously didn't ask questions about her competition piece; it was presumably still confined to studies in the drawing room, unless it was the one that had been covered as I came in.

As I made my way back home the sun was beginning to set, and with it went what warmth there was in the early Spring sun. So I walked briskly back along the lane and in the back gate into the park and down to the Abbey courtyard. As I crossed towards my door I saw activity in the inner courtyard, and looking through found Helena, Mark, Claudia, and Angela Carrington crowded round the back of a white van. I went to see if I could be of any assistance, as well as to satisfy my curiosity. I assumed at first that it was Declan from *Fishy Business*, but that wouldn't explain the excitement (unless he had started supplying something very exotic). But then I realised that it was a different sort of van, larger than Declan's. As I arrived at the back I saw that delivery men were removing two of the Blandings paintings, obviously returned from cleaning, and loading the next two into the van. All the paintings were of course professionally wrapped, and I was rather disappointed not to be able to see them.

'Oh Robbie, do come in while we unwrap the first Earl and take a look at him. I understand that he's been a great success. They've cleaned up the frame, too,' Helena said, mysteriously divining my wishes, as is her wont.

The van men had taken the painting that I assumed to be the Earl out of the van. They carried it carefully between them up the ramp to the back door of the Abbey, and then along the corridor and through the dining room and into the library. Ladders had already been placed on either side of the fireplace to facilitate its hanging. But first came the unwrapping. This is always a time-consuming process, and the restorer's men were very careful at it. At length there was only one layer of bubble-wrap left, and even through it we could see the warm glow of reds and yellows that had hardly been apparent in its previous, uncleaned state. When it was finally revealed, we all stood back to admire it before the job of re-hanging was undertaken. There was a gasp as we all took in what was now a riot of colour. The Earl's cape and decorations blazed out, the crimson of the drapery behind him setting off the blues, golds, silver and black in a perfection of harmony. In addition there was a lovely little dog at his feet which hadn't been visible before, and the chair and carpet were now revealed to be intricately detailed.

'Can it really be the same painting?' I asked, amazed; 'the colours are so vivid. I had no idea there were such bright colours used so long ago.'

'Oh, but of course, of course,' said Angela. 'Haven't you seen the before and after photographs of the Sistine Chapel? Many of the pigments that were used then are still used today, but the mediums have changed. And especially the varnishes. It was the horrible, old, yellowed and darkened varnish on this painting, together with the soot from years hanging over the fireplace, that made the painting so dull before. But the varnish that they have used now will not yellow, especially in this light. It can be cleaned of soot occasionally. And every fifty years the varnish can be removed and replaced.'

'It will be lucky to be replaced every hundred years,' said Helena, as the painting was carefully lifted into place.

'It's a good thing that the frame was cleaned as well;' I observed. 'It would have looked very shabby by contrast.' But now the gilt of the frame blazed as proudly as the colours of the painting. As it was straightened, the ladders were removed and we all stood back to see the total effect. To be honest, the rest of the library was rather lost in its presence.

'Don't anyone say it. I dare you to,' said Helena. 'I absolutely refuse even to contemplate redecorating the library.'

13

In the Abbey Garden

Spring had come, and with it a renewed optimism. The terrors of the winter were forgotten, and indeed seemed but a dream. For once early April was benign, and what with the blossom on the trees, the singing of nesting birds, and the shy appearance of tulips and bluebells among the late snowdrops and daffodils, everyone was out in their gardens with determination. We told ourselves that the winter had simply brought on a collective bout of jumpy nerves. It had begun to look as though Michael's murderer would never be discovered, and this fact bolstered our conviction that it was all a nasty incident in the past, and nothing to do with us. And so, Cathy was enjoying herself in the midst of her new compost, enthusiastically overseeing the renovation of herbaceous borders. Angela, I knew, was energetically pursuing her plans for her walled garden. There was now a new pond and paving, and she had recently made a small herb garden and planted a vine against the south-facing wall. Her chairs and table were ordered, and all that remained was to finish the plot where the bonfire debris had been, which was to be kept in flowers as a permanent memorial to Michael Slattery. As for me, Helena had shrewdly asked me to keep an eye on the cutting-flower garden. Because my sitting room overlooked it, it was in my own interest to find a balance between providing for the flower requirements of the

156

house, and leaving enough blooms on the shrubs and in the beds to ensure both a continuous supply of flowers, and constant colour in the garden. There were some very leggy rose bushes that needed particular attention. They produce beautiful, long-stemmed fragrant flowers, but are not attractive shrubs. With careful planning I had ensured that their lower halves would be hidden by herbaceous plants, which would themselves provide interesting flowers and foliage for arrangements. My efforts had already borne fruit in the form of Easter decorations for the church, which had looked particularly glorious this year.

It was therefore with mind, heart and hands cheerfully busy with the many tasks of a Spring garden that I had settled to work that day, under the cautious supervision of Theophrastes, curled up on my window ledge. And so it took some time for the gradually increasing sound of a siren to impinge on my consciousness. And even when it did, I was not at first alarmed to hear it stop on the other side of the Abbey, apparently in front of the Great Hall. 'Oh, dear,' I thought to myself absently. 'I wonder what's happened; has there been an accident?'

I soon became aware, however, that the commotion was urgent. By the sound of things, the vehicle had been an ambulance, and the crew had had to leave it in front of the Hall and continue into the gardens on foot. I waited for them to approach round the house and nearer to me, so that I might see what was happening, but instead their sound was growing fainter, heading toward the —

'What a fool I've been!' I shouted out loud, sending Theophrastes springing from his ledge. 'Cathy! Cathy!' I called wildly, hardly aware of rising and running to the gate of the garden. Fortunately I had brought the scooter round, to carry tools. Theophrastes and I dived at it as a single cat, and I frantically turned it and started off towards the ornamental gardens. Theophrastes was sitting upright in his basket, craning his neck forward, and thus obscuring my view. 'Anyone would think that you were in command of this vehicle,' I complained; 'Who do you think you are, Monty?'

It wasn't long, though, before I reached the public gardens and saw the ambulance crew in front of me. There they were, huddled round in a freshly dug border; a stretcher stood on the path in readiness. Two of the garden staff stood by, pale and nervous, absent-mindedly clutching a spade and a fork. I instinctively stopped and left the scooter before approaching softly, lest I distract the paramedics in any way. One of the gardeners spotted me, and, circumventing the ambulance team, came over to me. He had an obvious need to talk about what had happened, but no one had yet had time to hear him. 'It don't make sense,' he said. 'We'd been digging in the new compost from that big new machine. We've been at it all morning. Mrs Baskerville was supervising, as usual, telling us which beds to dig over. We'd lifted the clumps here yesterday,' he said, indicating a prodigious quantity of herbaceous matter, already divided and ready for replanting. 'There was nothing happening at all. If anything, Mrs Baskerville has been much better of late; her new knee is going grand, so. And we were all just chatting away, like, talking about how to arrange things in the new soil. And she was that proud of it; she was bent down running her fingers through it, when we heard her gasp sudden, and the next thing she was over in the muck, her face all purple, and fighting for breath. We turned her over to be more comfortable, you know, and then I phoned Max, and he phoned the emergency, and here they are, so;' he concluded, looking round worriedly at Cathy, who was now being lifted carefully onto the stretcher.

'Where is Mrs Chancellor?' I asked.

'In Rathcoole, doing her shopping.'

I went over to Cathy as they carefully strapped her onto the stretcher, in preparation for taking her to the ambulance. Her eyes were open, and she was no longer purple, though her face was still a bad colour, and her heart was racing. Her breathing was shallow, and her voice was weak. 'Oh, dear Robbie,' she said, seeing me; 'So sorry, such a fuss.'

'Now, don't be silly and start worrying about us, old thing,' I said; although I'm afraid that my voice was trembling. 'You're in good hands, now, and we'll have you out again in no time.'

The ambulance crew was now waiting to take the stretcher, and I began to straighten up to back away. But 'Oh, Robbie,' I heard Cathy say, and looking at her I saw a heart-breaking, pleading expression in her eyes. I instinctively took her hands, and felt something hard being pressed into mine. 'Please,' she said, as she was moved off to the ambulance. There was the sound of the quad bike coming from the forest; Billy had obviously been informed by Max, and was coming to see what was happening. As the gardeners moved towards him, I took the opportunity to glance at the object in my hands; and there, covered in compost, was a set of human teeth. I hurriedly wrapped them in a handkerchief and thrust them into a pocket as Billy approached me, followed by the gardeners, both of whom were speaking rapidly about the incident.

'Hello, Robbie,' he said. 'I'm really sorry about this; does she have a history of heart trouble?'

I replied that, as far as I knew, Cathy had a very strong constitution. We chatted for a few minutes, while I attempted to appear calm and natural. But as soon as it seemed appropriate to do so, I took my leave, and made my way home to telephone the Guards.

'But why weren't the teeth broken down in the digester, along with the other bones? It seems bizarre that they should have survived, and attached to the jaws.' It was proving difficult to explain things to Helena; and indeed that was hardly surprising, given the unusual circumstances. She had arrived back from her outing to Rathcoole to find Garda forensic teams once more in occupation of part of the estate, this time much closer to the house. It was only to be expected that she would be exasperated, and less than usually attentive to explanations.

'No, no — I'm afraid that I haven't put things properly. The teeth that Cathy found weren't real teeth, and they weren't attached to the jaw. It seems that they are state of the art dentures, made of the same materials as are used in the best tooth implants. I assume that when Cathy found them, she remembered how Dickie had boasted to her that he was having implants made; you remember her telling us that at Christmas? She said that he had had all his remaining teeth extracted, and dentures made, pending his visit to Indonesia for implants. And so she probably assumed, as soon as she saw them, that these dentures were his, and that if they were in the compost from the digester. . .'

'What a terrible shock for her! I do hope they leave her alone until she has quite recovered,' said Helena. 'But are they very sure that anything more of Dickie was put into the composter? Perhaps he simply lost his dentures, and someone threw them into one of the recycling bins; though I grant you that would be an odd thing to do. Or perhaps they're someone else's; I mean, he isn't the only person to wear dentures, is he?'

'No, but it's the sort of thing that one would notice, isn't it?' I countered. 'It's not like going for a walk without one's reading glasses. I've never heard of anyone forgetting that they hadn't their dentures in. Not any live person, anyway. And a live person who lost dentures would surely raise the alarm and ask for help in finding them, however embarrassing that might be. As

161

for the question of a body having been put into the compost digester, I can only point out that the Guards have been taking things away from the border in bags for analysis. They're not saying anything, of course, but they seem at least to be taking the possibility seriously that Dickie's — or someone's — remains were in the compost. And besides, Dickie is the only one who has been missing; they know that perfectly well, since they were called in to look for him. Dickie wore dentures, and has been missing long enough to have been composted. Of course, it might all turn out to be a mare's nest, but what I'm saying is that if Cathy thought along those lines, it would explain her collapse.'

'Yes, I can see that,' said Helena. 'What a grizzly turn of events. Just when I thought we were out of the headlines and could return to something like normal. The gardens ought to be re-opening next month to the public, but now I'm not sure what to do. On the one hand I don't want to contribute to the drama, but on the other hand I really don't want crowds of sensation seekers coming to see the border. I'll have to speak to William about it, if I can find him; he's somewhere in Africa at the moment.'

'Goodness, what's he looking for there?' I asked, diverted for a moment from the serious business in hand.

'Bio-fuels. There are some grasses that might be suitable to grow here, like elephant grass, but easier to harvest. We were thinking of devoting part of a field to experimenting with them. I just hope nothing small comes back with him in a jar as well. I don't think that I could cope with planning an African pond, certainly not at the moment — though we do have a few baobab saplings in the greenhouse, now that I think about it.

'Do you know,' Helena continued, 'I wouldn't put it past Dickie to have thrown his dentures into the composter himself, and run off somewhere. I know we found his passport when we looked into his flat at Christmas, but he might easily have another.'

'But *why*?' I countered. 'That's just what doesn't make sense of any of this. We still have no indication of anything criminal having taken place before Michael Slattery's death; so why murder him? And we haven't any suggestion of anything criminal having taken place, apart from Michael's murder, up to the present. There have been no suggestions of Dickie being wanted for anything dodgy, so why run away? It's an awfully extreme thing to do. And I'm afraid that, although I can easily believe that Dickie might have done business to within a hair's breadth of the limits of the law (if not beyond them), I really can't imagine him ever resorting to physical violence of any kind, let alone murder. And in any case, we come back to the question of why he would have wanted to kill Michael?'

'And why would anyone want to kill Dickie?' pursued Helena. 'Well, it's all beyond me, I'm afraid. I just hope that the Guards will hurry up and sort it all out. And I don't mind admitting that I'd like it all cleared up before the gardens are due to open. Or at the very least, before the twinning festivities.'

'Good Lord, yes!' I exclaimed. 'Do you know, what with Easter, and the good weather, and now this, I had forgotten all about it. I didn't know that everything was agreed on and that dates had been set.'

'Oh yes, it's all set for midsummer's eve; and I, for my sins, have volunteered the Great Hall and the park for the festivities. It's curious, but I have found over the years that if you volunteer a castle as a venue, no one ever declines it. I can't remember exactly how I got roped into this one. It seemed to be a combined effort by Mark, Claudia, Angela, and Fr Enda. And of course Penny was all for it. Only Mr Moto seemed a bit cool about it; I gather that he feels that we should take things like midsummer more seriously, in a Druidic sort of way. I daresay he'll find someplace megalithic where he can spend his day with greater artistic verisimilitude. I wonder whether I could go with him? But I suppose I'll be wanted here to shake hands with people.'

'What's the name again of the town that Ardliss is to be twinned with?' I asked.

'Santa Maria degli Angeli,' replied Helena. 'I gather that it is Claudia Crespi's home town, not far from Rome. Angela and Enda have been to see it, and came back full of its praises. And Mark of course considers it to be a Renaissance treasure. Is there any place in Italy that *isn't* a Renaissance treasure?' she added, and I could see that her temper was becoming frayed. I therefore took my leave, and went in search of information about where Cathy had been taken, and when she would be allowed visitors. I knew that the Guards would be the first to see her, and like Helena, I hoped that they wouldn't distress her.

Happily, it was a mere matter of days before Cathy was allowed visitors. There being little that she could tell the Guards that hadn't been deduced already, she was recovering rapidly and was expected to be released within a week or so. I had expected to be one of the first to call on her, but entering her room I found that I had to wade through an exotic garden of hothouse flowers, chocolates and gardening magazines. I felt rather ashamed of my modest gift of grapes. Hearing me enter, Cathy glanced up from a book and beamed at me. 'Grapes!' she exclaimed. 'What a treat. You know, I have no idea how I'm going to get through all this chocolate. I can't very well give it away, either. Perhaps when I get out I should throw a chocolate party.'

It did my heart good to see her back in form, and we sat happily together for a while, chatting and picking at the grapes. 'You must think me rather dilatory to be behind so many others in visiting you,' I said. 'I only found out today that you could receive visitors. Who else has been here?'

'Oh, the world and his wife, really;' she replied. 'They started coming yesterday. Some of them I hardly know. They all came bearing gifts and commiserations, obviously hoping that I'd feel like chatting about dentures. Which I didn't.'

'That really is too much!' I said indignantly. 'People can be dreadful. Didn't it occur to them that you need to rest?'

'Well, I didn't actually mind. To tell you the truth, I'm getting rather bored. I'd like to be out and back in the garden while the weather lasts.'

'Now, you're to take it easy, my dear!' I said. 'This will all have taken more out of you than perhaps you feel!' I saw that she had already been rummaging in the gardening magazines and seed catalogues. I looked at the book that she had been reading when I arrived. 'Cathy!' I exclaimed. 'What on earth are you doing reading this sort of thing? It can hardly be good for your heart.' The book was in fact *Appointment with Death* by Agatha Christie. Imagine Cathy sitting in hospital reading murder mysteries after such a shock!

'Well, to tell you the truth,' she said, 'I find myself thinking of murders anyway. I simply can't understand how Dickie can have been murdered, or why or by whom. It all keeps going round and round in my head. It was beginning to make me feverish, and I had to do something. It occurred to me that I might be able to drive out one murder with another, and I started reading this one. Do you know, it really is rather good! Have you read it?'

I confessed that I had not.

'Well, you should. It's got me fascinated. In a way it's the opposite of our problems, because we can't work out why anyone is killing people, whereas in this book you could understand anyone killing that old dragon. There are so many suspects, but always the same motive. But you hope that it won't be one of the family, because you've come to care for them, you know. It's very diverting. I think when I finish this one I'll read another.'

I could hardly feel that this was healthy, and so I brought out my real present and presented it to her. Opening the envelope she saw that I had ordered several fruit trees for her.

'They'll be arriving in the next week, so you had better start thinking about where you will want them!' I said, as her eyes widened in anticipation. 'If you decided to put one of the cherries in the cutting-flower garden, I must say that I wouldn't mind.'

'Oh Robbie, how good of you! But only a week to plan for them. Have you put the garden staff on alert?'

'Of course,' I said, pleased that the gift had been a success. 'There isn't meant to be any work involved in this for you at all. You just decide where you want them, and we'll see to the rest.'

'They must be container planted if they're coming this time of year,' she said.

'Yes,' I confessed, 'I thought that would be the best thing. It's really too late for bare-root planting. So there's no rush to get them in.'

'Good! That will give me time to finish my book.'

And so I was able to leave the hospital knowing that Cathy was happily recovering among her gardening magazines and murder mysteries. Until the Guards informed us of the results of their forensic inquiries, there was nothing more to be done but wait, and keep gardening. For the first time I could remember, I felt less than delighted at the prospect, knowing that murder would be going round and round in my head, too.

14
The Easter General Vestry

It was with a degree of psychological exertion that, in the following week, Matthew sat down to prepare the agenda for the Easter General Vestry. He could not help himself feeling relieved that Easter itself had been celebrated before the discovery of Dickie's remains. 'Well, I'm sorry for you,' Enda had said, with reference to the complicated business of the funeral. Most of Dickie Bird had been mixed in with the rest of the compost from the 'digester', and a lot of that had already been dug into the ornamental flower garden before his teeth had been discovered. 'At least they weren't digging over the vegetable garden at the time,' Helena had sensibly observed. 'People can be squeamish about that sort of thing. Not that it ought to matter really, nitrogen being nitrogen, but on the other hand you can understand. But flowers are somehow appropriate.' And so in the end it had been decided that Dickie's funeral would take place with the forensic samples, when they were returned. There could hardly be a removal, though Helena had thoughtfully offered to have the new compost dug out and delivered to the churchyard. In the end it had been agreed between Matthew and Helena (Dickie having no living relations) that after the funeral the forensic matter would be brought to the flower bed at Blandings which held the rest of his remains, interred there, and the entire border dedicated as his memorial as well as his grave. One of the things Matthew intended to mention at the Vestry meeting was an invitation for anyone to contribute whatever herbaceous or shrubby plants they might care to, from a list supplied by Cathy. 'That's the second memorial garden we have in the parish now,' Angela had remarked. 'I hope it's not going to become a fashion.'

'We'll insist that it's only for murder victims,' Matthew had replied.

'That's what I mean,' she retorted.

Looking out of his study window, Matthew saw that the warm evening, following a week of intermittent rain, had resulted in a gathering fog. By the time he was ready to set out to the church hall he could hardly see as far as the hedge that divided the front garden from the Rectory field, even though the sun hadn't yet set. 'I don't suppose that many people will turn out, given the weather.' Matthew said to Angela as she helped him into his coat. 'You won't be late, will you?'

'Am I ever late? As soon as I've washed the dishes I'll be over. There's no need for me to sit there watching you and Rosie putting out chairs.'

As he crossed the Rectory field the outline of the hall grew more distinct before him. 'That's odd,' he thought, seeing the shapes of cars grow in clarity in the car park. It is Matthew's habit to arrive well in advance of Vestry meetings, to help Rosie Donahoe set up, and to talk the agenda through with her before the others appear. But by the time he reached the door he realised that the car park was full; and as he entered the hall he was assailed by a throng of voices. 'Good Lord!' he exclaimed, despite himself. As he adjusted to the sight of the multitude seated in animated discussion before the podium, Rosie came up to him.

'They started arriving around seven,' she said. 'Some were waiting for me when I got here to put on the heat.'

'But why?' asked Matthew.

'Well, I suppose they're concerned about all these murders.'

Passing over the fact that two murders hardly constitute 'all these', Matthew said, 'But that's not what the meeting is about! I know that there are no elections to take place this year, but this is still a Vestry meeting, and we have parish business to discuss.'

'Well . . .' said Rosie doubtfully.

'Are you sure they're all on the electoral roll?' he asked, eyeing the crowd dubiously. 'I'm convinced that there are faces here that I don't recognise.'

'Oh, yes' she said with decision. 'I've watched them all coming in. Mind you, some of them have only come on this year.'

'Well, that's good!' he said.

'I suppose everyone wants to make sure they've got a place to be buried in, just in case,' she continued.

Matthew decided to ignore this.

Aware that his presence on the podium would effectively start proceedings, Matthew remained by the door with Rosie as more people arrived. When Angela came in she shot an alarmed glance at Matthew, before finding a seat near the door. 'Just like an Italian,' he thought to himself bitterly. 'They all have an inbuilt instinct for making sure they're near an escape route.' *'Don't leave early!'* he hissed in her ear. She looked at him enigmatically. At last it could be delayed no longer, and he made his way to the podium, as the Treasurer and Secretary followed him. Silence fell. 'Let us pray,' he began.

With the opening prayers, welcome and introduction over, agendas were distributed in silence. 'It's alright after all', he thought innocently, not recognising the calm before a storm. Apologies, minutes of the last meeting, and amendments to the electoral roll went through without a murmur. It was therefore with confidence that Matthew turned to the Treasurer's Report. Apart from the need to keep an eye on fund raising, there was nothing contentious in that. Indeed, the financial report was as mind-numbing as ever, though the church wardens did their best to scrutinise the Treasurer. Fund raising was, as ever, the great concern, since it emerged that we had once again fallen short by over a thousand euros over the year.

'What about selling that field between Noyestown and Greenborough?' someone suggested. 'It should make a fair bit for development.'

'What would it be developed for?' someone else asked.

'They could build a hotel on it for the new watersports centre on Lough Coile,' said someone else.

'Well then we could build our own hotel, and get the money out of it ourselves.'

'Is that water sports centre still going ahead?' asked someone.

Oh, yes; I've heard that they're going to build a big casino in the middle of the lake, with holiday chalets built out over the water on stilts.' said yet another voice.

'No, no; that was before Christmas! I heard this week that they're selling the whole lake to Buddhists. It's a big temple that's to be built in the middle of the lake. And it's their own huts that are to be built out over the lake, the way Oriental people like to. And they're to have their own airport as well, as big as Knock.'

'Oh, that would be good,' said someone else. 'Where will you be able to fly to?'

'Buddhist places, I suppose.'

'What sort of a hotel would Buddhists be wanting, then?'

'Perhaps we could sell the field to them for their airport.'

'I don't think it's big enough.'

Struggling to grasp this runaway horse, Matthew interjected, 'Look, we can't build hotels, let alone run them, for Buddhists or anyone else. We really can't get involved at all in whatever development may or may not be happening around the lake. Of course we have the option of selling the field, as long as we are sure that the use it's put to will be in the interests of the community. But we must think very carefully before deciding to sell any of our assets, and even then we might not be given

173

permission to do so. Our fundraising shortfall is not so great that we have to think about selling land.'

But 'Maybe we could sell it as arable,' someone persisted. 'I've heard that the people who now own the field beside the school have got a license to experiment with GM wheat. Maybe someone would want to grow GM in our field.' At this there was an alarmed murmur.

'But that would be terrible!' several voices replied.

'No, no; it's that elephant grass that they're going to do a trial of in the field beside the school,' said a voice.

'Well, we could do that ourselves, without selling our field. Maybe we should keep it, and grow elephant grass ourselves. It's meant to be the most amazing bio-fuel, with little or no trouble after the initial sowing.'

'We could supply the whole parish with electricity!' said someone enthusiastically.

'I've heard it's from the Himalayas; it would make the Buddhists feel at home.'

With rising exasperation, Matthew called the meeting back to order. 'We really must avoid speculating about Buddhists. I have no reason to believe that the lake has been sold to Buddhists or to anyone else; I'm not even certain how much of it is private property, or who owns it if it is. And in any case, we can't start thinking now about a parish co-operative to grow elephant grass. Apart from anything else, its development is still in the planning stages. It will require special facilities for preparing it, as well as for burning it. We must think of one thing at a time, and right now we're discussing how best to increase our fundraising by more conventional means.'

But as Matthew was taking a deep breath to continue, someone said, 'Who does own the field by the school, now that Michael Slattery and Dick Bird are dead?'

'I have no information on who owns Dickie's half of the field;' Matthew said, forestalling any other interruptions. 'But Sinead Slattery still owns her half, and I think we can feel confident that she will not allow anything detrimental to the interests of the community to be done to the field. In any case, that is not the business of this meeting. To continue, I have received several suggestions for additional fundraising activities that we might undertake . . .'

'At least someone has made sure that that housing development can't go ahead,' said a voice; and suddenly everyone was talking at once. It was in vain that Matthew tried to gain the upper hand.

'Is that why they were killed? To stop them building all them houses?'

'No, it was to stop them building the golf course.'

'I heard that it was so that the field would have to be sold, so that someone else could buy it for development.'

'No, no — you mean whoever wants to grow that GM wheat.'

'Whoever buys that field, that will be who killed them!'

THE SERPENT IN THE GARDEN

'I don't believe it's anything to do with the field. That's what they want us to think! Haven't you heard that paintings have been disappearing from the Abbey? There were three of them in it, and now there's only one left, he can take all the profit.'

'But they're being cleaned!' exclaimed Angela, despite her determination to remain invisible.

'Ah, but how do we know that? How do we know that they weren't to be sold on through the Slatterys' antique shop in Dublin?'

Angela was tempted to try to explain that it would be all but impossible to do such a thing, but decided that it was best to give up an unequal struggle.

'I don't think it has anything to do with that sort of thing at all. Sure we all know that the pair of them took bets down to the races. It's organised crime; something was passing hands somewhere, for something.'

'Is it true that Steve Blackmore has lost his licence?' said someone. There was an appalled silence, followed by a censorious gasp. Cries of 'Shame!' came from various directions.

'*That's a lie!*' cried a small voice out of the crowd. It was Lucy, poor dear; no one had noticed her, sitting at the back. But there she was, white lipped and pale faced, her fists clenched in her lap. The multitude turned upon the slanderer, who, red from ear to ear, made his abject apologies to her. But it was an ugly incident, and the poor child was obviously near to tears. There was a sobered hush, as people recollected themselves.

'We are here,' said Matthew, valiantly seizing the opportunity to return to the agenda, 'to discuss parish business, and most importantly to plan this year's *fête*. As you all know, this summer it will form part of the celebrations for the twinning of Ardliss with Santa Maria degli Angeli, in Lazio, Italy. There will be several dignitaries present; the Ambassador of Italy, the Papal Nuncio, and the *Taoiseach*, among others. So it is a real chance to raise the profile of the parish, as well as to raise funds. For this reason it will be much larger than usual, with several new events. The most important of these will be the barbecue and disco, which still have to be organised. The pony rides will be extended into proper lessons, since the Pony Club has agreed to come on here after their demonstration at the Abbey.'

'But aren't they selling the Abbey to Walt Disney for a theme park?' asked Mrs Shaw. 'When does that happen, before or after the twinning?'

'No, no, no — it's that they're making a big Hollywood film there, about Oliver Cromwell,' said a churchwarden.

'Who's in it?' said a voice from the back.

'George Clooney and Nicole Kidman,' said the churchwarden, with the pride of prior knowledge.

'*Oooh*!' responded the assembled multitude.

'They can hardly be having George Clooney playing Cromwell. They would need someone ugly for that,' reflected the glebe warden.

'Robbie and I will do the barbeque,' said Cathy, throwing herself manfully into the breach. Her recovery had been rapid, and here she was, seemingly as fit as ever. But I wasn't convinced that barbecue organising was really the best thing for her. I had unearthed the two-seater from its winter hibernation in honour of her homecoming, and this was her first real outing.

'Hear, hear!' I answered in my confusion; 'I mean to say, of course we shall!' — although I wasn't at all certain how; my culinary skills being limited to preparing a light meal for a few friends.

'I'm doing that,' said Louise, who is a professional caterer.

'Yes, and we're very grateful,' said Matthew (to say nothing of how grateful I was!). 'But there are still the tickets and beverages to arrange.'

'Cathy and I will do drinks,' I said. Why should she be the only one to volunteer our combined efforts?

'Thank you very much, Robbie, Cathy' said Matthew. 'We're getting quotations for the printing of the tickets, and then it will be up to us all to sell them. The other thing we have to think about is how to bring the marquee down from Noyestown to the Rectory field.'

'Well, I'm not going down the bog road again until the bishop comes and exorcises the ghosts off it,' said Mr Smith. There was a pause.

'Do we believe in that?' asked the glebe warden.

'We do,' said Mrs Smith, with decision. 'I heard the Archbishop of Canterbury talking about it on the radio.'

Someone asked, 'Does that mean that it's in Sharia Law then?' There was another pause.

'But do we have exorcism in the Church of Ireland?' persisted the glebe warden, looking accusingly at Matthew, whose head had sunk into his hands.

'Well, we need to do something, before we're all murdered in our beds!' countered Mr Smith.

At this there was a cacophony of voices.

'*Now stop this*!' Matthew's voice boomed above the noise, and there was a hush. 'We really mustn't get things out of perspective,' he continued calmly. 'These unfortunate — these appalling and despicable murders, have nothing whatsoever to do with the parish. There has been no suggestion made by the Guards that they have anything to do with any of us at all. There can therefore be no danger posed to anyone innocent. All we need to ensure is that we tell the police promptly about anything we might know. It is obvious from both murders that they have some connection with illegal practices; therefore honest people should feel completely safe.'

At this, there was such a silence as would have allowed a dropped pin to be heard. The soul-searching was palpable.

'I agreed to throw in some extra honey if I could have exclusive rights as their jam supplier.'

'I agreed to accept free silage if I allowed that field to be included for his Area Aid.'

'I went the wrong way round the one way system on my way to church last Sunday.'

'I said I would give free Italian lessons in return for canvases and brushes.'

Everyone present was examining his heart in case his slide into temptation had been great enough to draw him into the murky underworld of homicidal crime.

'We also need to decide whether it will be necessary to hire a professional disc jockey for the disco, or whether we think we can manage it ourselves.' Matthew's voice stirred us all from our thoughts.

'I'll have a go, if someone else will help me.' It was Lucy, plucky as usual, and she blushed at the thanks and applause she received.

'I'll help,' said Andrew, a generally shy young man of about Lucy's age. 'But I don't know much about it.'

'Well, we've time to work it out,' said Lucy.

'Thank you both very much,' said Matthew, as everyone else chimed in. It seemed that we had recovered our equilibrium, and the rest of the meeting went without incident. But as we were leaving, I looked at the fog drifting in billows through the night, and wondered how many of the parishioners from around Noyestown would be taking the bog road home that night.

15
The Gathering Storm

Summer came at last, and with it an infectious cheerfulness. Dickie's memorial border was commemorated in May, with the interment of his forensic remains in the midst of it. Cathy had put her best efforts into planning something special, and I must say that the people of the parish were very generous in supplying her with the items she had requested. Unlike most borders, this one was not to be subject to the regular lifting and division required by herbaceous plants. At the back, therefore, Cathy had rather informally planted several English roses, blending Summer Song with Pat Austin and Christopher Marlowe for warmth. Amongst them were a low-growing, variegated *pittosporum*, and a beautiful variety of silver lavender. The cool tones of these made for a delicious contrast with the apricots and oranges of the roses. Then there were skimmias, and *vinca*, and Byzantine lilies, and heaven knows what else. The only concession made to clump-forming plants was an orange *papaver orientale*, which, once summer came and it blossomed, put the final touch on a beautifully conceived display.

I was myself of course engrossed in the cutting-flower garden, as well as spending an increasing amount of time at the Blackmores' yard. I had indeed begun during May to find ever-increasing pretexts for being busy, absent, or generally invisible. This was not due to any newly developed misanthropy, but to the pernicious tendency of the twinning committee to overwhelm everything and everyone in its wake. Poor Dickie's service was indeed the only respite I could remember during the month from the invasive presence of committee members, who seemed to have fixed ideas about all the useful things everyone might be able to do to forward preparations. Having two members of the committee actually living at the Abbey, and another next door at the Rectory, made this a particular problem for Penny, Cathy and me. The Avakians were spared out of tact; and it was unreasonable to expect Mr Moto to feel any interest in the project.

This isn't to suggest that Penny, Cathy and I were unwilling to pull our weight in the combined community effort; it was just that, once one agreed to do a thing, it had a way of turning into ten things. To look too willing would have been to offer oneself as a living victim. The three of us had therefore hit upon a scheme for staying in covert communication with each other, and operated a form of intelligence network for our mutual protection. The idea arose from the fact that young Bobby Baskerville, Cathy's eight-year-old grandson, had given her an all-singing, all-dancing mobile telephone for Christmas. This had remained in its box until Bobby had found time to show her how to use it. As a result, almost no one knew her number, and few people even knew of the existence of the instrument. As the threat of the twinners became more acute, we three had met in committee and decided that Penny and I should each purchase an identical phone to Cathy's, which she could then teach us to use. And so it was that we were able to go to ground in the gardens as need arose, and warn each other of any impending danger.

I have to confess that, having taken the step to purchase one of these phones as a matter of necessity, I soon realised that a whole new world had opened up for me. As a professional scholar, the only concession I had already made to micro-technology was my Macintosh notebook. And since the only electronic communication I regularly undertook was to e-mail articles and proofs to publishers, I had always made do with a telephone internet connection. Now, as readers will be aware, with these phones one is able not only to speak to, but also to see one's interlocutor. It is also possible to take photographs with the tiny instrument. And so, having lost all self-control and subscribed to broadband, I found that I could also send these photographs to friends, and to other horticultural enthusiasts. Thus the whole world of the internet gradually opened to me, as I took to making regular checks on world news, as well as weather forecasts, via both the computer and the little phone. But it took us all a while to realise that we could all three speak to each other at the same time. And I'm afraid that that really did lead us into temptation, since we could now (instead of getting properly dressed to meet for a chat of an evening) have a good gossip and update on affairs while we were each seated comfortably with our ovaltine (or whatever) in front of our own fires.

But we all bore in mind the danger of being overheard; I believe that security on this front is still imperfect.

Meanwhile, from the safety of our defensive positions, we were aware of twinning activity all around us. The representatives from Santa Maria degli Angeli were to be hosted during the week of their stay by various local families. Our local TD was to look after the Italian mayor, and Fr Enda would be accommodating his opposite number from the Italian parish. Various local outings were being arranged for the party from the Monday to the Friday, which didn't impinge on us, fortunately. Formal community festivities were to commence on Saturday with a hurling demonstration in the morning, the Church of Ireland parish *fête* in the afternoon, followed by the disco. Sunday morning the dignitaries would arrive in time for Mass, where the parish priest of Santa Maria degli Angeli would concelebrate with Fr Enda, and the Apostolic Nuncio (himself an Italian) would give the homily. There would follow a communal lunch in the Community Centre, which both congregations would attend. This was to be organised by Fr Enda's parishioners, with copious provision of delicacies from Santa Maria degli Angeli. There would be traditional Irish music and Irish dancing to conclude.

So far, so good. Cathy and I had been let off the hook with regards to serving drinks at the parish barbecue, since the Italians would thoughtfully be arriving with unnumbered gallons of their local wines (selected with the careful assistance of Fr Enda), which they intended to serve themselves at both the *fête* barbecue and Sunday lunch. But Sunday afternoon, after the communal lunch and entertainment, the whole event was to arrive among us. The afternoon itself was to be given over to a gymkhana and point-to-point races on the estate, which were to serve as a festive backdrop to the serious business of displays of local industry and produce. In the evening would follow an organ and harp concert. After that would come the welcoming speeches, and then a formal dinner in the Abbey for the dignitaries, respective planning committees, and others who had given their time to the project. And finally, to conclude it all, in the twilight of Midsummer Eve there was to be a fireworks display.

I think that I have already explained, in the early stages of this narrative, that Blandings is not really a very 'horsey' estate. It is in fact more 'cow-y' and 'wheat-y'. It was thus by a fortuitous combination of circumstances that the twinning celebrations were to take place during a fortnight's pause between the harvesting of one Blandings crop and the sowing of the next. And this is why it was possible to stage a demonstration 'point-to-point' on the estate, which was generally not given to hosting equestrian events. It was thought that this sort of display would interest our guests (and, to be honest, any excuse would do). The equestrian activities, quite reasonably, did not involve Helena, except to the extent of her giving permission for them, and approving their details. In the same way, Max and Billy were not too put upon for their efforts, though Billy (being a true

Kiwi, and fond of horses), volunteered to assist with route planning and course marking for the races, and the construction of fences. Cathy for her part had the not inconsiderable responsibility of ensuring that the gardens were at their best. And Penny, although theoretically a sitting target in the tea-room, was in charge of planning and supervising the dinner in the Great Hall. She was thus enabled, by the necessary employment of auxiliaries, to beat a hasty retreat into the gardens when the enemy were known to be advancing upon the tea-room or kitchen.

Of all of us, therefore, I was the most lightly defended. Apart from ensuring that the cutting-flower garden was up to supplying the house for the concert and dinner, I could be considered to be 'unoccupied'. I was therefore captive prey among the flowers for anyone who appeared bearing leaflets, posters, raffle tickets, balloons, flags and bunting, or requesting flowers, cakes, bottles or white elephants for stalls. When these requests manifested themselves in the company of committee members, there was the additional trial of moral blackmail, with the suggestion that those who had been particularly 'helpful' with organisation would be considered for inclusion in the reciprocal party which was to be welcomed to Santa Maria degli Angeli in September. It was therefore I of the three of us who benefitted most from our mobile coms network.

I dare say that I am giving the impression that I lack team spirit; but this has to be seen in context. In other circumstances I would have been only too willing

186

to help with the donkey work that forms the bulk of preparations for all such events. But in this case, I considered my loyalties to lie elsewhere. Although the unofficial 'point-to-point' was being organised by the hunt, and the gymkhana by the Pony Club, it transpired that Lucy Blackmore had come in for a great deal more than her fair share of work. She was, of course, responsible with Andrew for the music for the disco on Saturday night, and it was impossible to predict how long that would last. But then the next day she would be bringing up horses from the livery and eventing yard where she worked, overseeing stable lines, feed and water, and preparing her novices for their race as well as participating in her own. I couldn't see that she would be getting any rest between these activities, never mind being able to share in any of the festivities. To all this was added the strain of keeping an eye on her sister Alice, and little Bobby Baskerville. Bobby was inclined to think the Pony Club beneath him, and he was easily capable of arriving on a borrowed 'pony' that was every finger of 15hh. There are always little imps to keep an eye on, but Bobby was in a class by himself. It was particularly hard on Lucy to have to police Alice, since she was now the nearest to a mother that the poor girl had, and Lucy disliked any tension to arise between them. In order to placate her, therefore, and the other young thrusters, Lucy had hit upon the idea of holding junior races, just for them. Since the races were not an official point-to-point, it was at the discretion of the hunt to devise them in any way thought suitable. Therefore

Alice's race was to be 'fly-weight', thus preserving the dignity of competitors. Then little Bobby started kicking up, and we ended up committed to a 'gnat-weight', flat race as well ('flea-weight' having a rather pejorative sound).

It was for all these reasons, then, that I decided to devote what energy and free time I had to taking as much work off Lucy's shoulders as I could. I was particularly well placed to suggest suitable venues for stabling, and for race routes that would avoid any disastrous encounters with flowers, fruit trees, elderly tenants, cows or llamas. I had decided against speaking to Steve about the extent of Lucy's commitment. He was under a lot of pressure himself, as usual, and besides, Lucy was an adult. It doesn't do to interfere between parents and children, even when one is a close friend. So I was pleased, though not really surprised, when I heard that a mystery donor had provided for the hiring of a professional disc jockey for the *fête*. It was by far the best thing for everyone. Andrew was pleased to be able to attend the event with his girl friend, Lucy was relieved at the prospect of a good night's sleep, and the disco could be advertised as a professionally run event.

Billy was, as I have indicated, a great help with course building, and quite frequently I found myself taking the scooter round to his house in off-hours for consultations and updates. He had agreed to help with looking after stable lines and calling riders forward on the day. And he was fully entitled to give as much time on the day as he cared to, it being a free Sunday for him.

But I sensed that Max was growing increasingly irritated at the intrusion of the festival into the routine of the farm. Although the harvest was in, and the straw baled, a dairy herd has to continue its life uninterrupted. It was inevitable that most of the race routes would have to go over grazing meadow, and though it was left to Max to decide which of the fields were to be incorporated, cattle need to be rotated, and it was bound to make extra work for him. At times his vetoes on a route passing through this or that part of the farm began to seem obstructive. And he particularly resented all the calls that were being made for Billy's assistance — at times, I thought, unreasonably. And so I am afraid that he began to look upon me rather as an outrider of the impending equine invasion.

It gradually came about, therefore, that I got into the habit of approaching the cottages by Debbie's stable block with a degree of circumspection. Max was usually to be found in or around one or other of the farm offices, but there was nothing to stop him from nipping home for a cup of tea, so to speak. And if he did come home unexpectedly, I didn't want him to see me chatting with Billy, and accuse him of doing private business on company time, as it were. But there were inevitably times when I had a quick question for Billy that couldn't be explained by phone. If it was anywhere near a break time for him, we would generally agree to meet for a few minutes when he was free, either *in situ* (if it was a question concerning the course), or if it was in the evening, back at his house, where we could have a cup of something together.

And so it was that, on one evening about a fortnight before the event, I found myself on the scooter, riding along the lane, in much the same way that I had on that evening nearly a year before, when I had visited Debbie to see where Michael's murder weapon had been discovered. It was disconcerting to think that so much time had passed and yet we were no nearer solving that mystery. As I drew nearer I dismounted and left the scooter some way from Debbie's studio and the Slatterys' house (it has rather a distinctive sound, and there was no point in drawing undue attention to my presence). Again as on that previous occasion, Sinead and the boys seemed to be away. She was of course having to spend an increasing amount of time in Dublin, and was unwilling to have the children away from her for more time than was necessary. I suspected that it wouldn't be long before she found it more convenient to live nearer to the city. The surrounding landscape as I drew near Debbie's gate was lit by the lovely, subdued light that is unique to northern summer evenings, and Venus shone as brightly as a flame, although the sun was still long from setting. As I was passing the stables gate, though, I was startled and surprised to hear raised voices coming from the studio. I paused to listen. There was silence. But as I stood irresolute, unsure whether to ignore what was obviously none of my business, or to go and check that everything was alright, I heard the door of the studio open violently. I instinctively drew back behind the wall, as I heard Debbie's voice saying, 'So that's all the thanks I get, then, for keeping your secrets. All I wanted was a small favour. It would have made my life a lot easier, and not done you any harm at all.'

'I've had altogether enough favours asked of me lately; and I don't owe you anything,' I heard Max reply. 'All that's over now, and besides, you couldn't prove anything, could you? It would just be your word against mine.'

At this the door slammed shut, and I'm afraid that I suffered the indignity of scrambling into the hedge in front of the Slatterys' house in order to avoid the embarrassment of encountering Max as he came into the lane. The sight of me there would have irritated him in any event, without the added annoyance of knowing that I had overheard what was obviously a personal row. I glanced back down the lane to where I had left the scooter. I had taken no pains to conceal it, and it was plainly visible. Fortunately, however, Max turned the other direction, and strode off rapidly towards his house. Under the circumstances, I thought it best to ring Billy and call off our meeting. As I emerged from the hedge, dusting myself off and checking that the coast was clear, on impulse I decided to go and knock on Debbie's door. She opened it without a word, possibly expecting it to be Max again. When she saw me her face fell. Not wishing to dissemble, and already ashamed of myself for letting my curiosity compel me to intrude upon her, I fell back upon that best of all stratagems: truth.

'I'm sorry if I'm intruding,' I said, 'but I heard raised voices as I was passing, and then I saw Max leaving, looking rather angry. So I've taken the liberty of coming to see that everything is alright.'

At this she started uneasily, obviously wondering whether I had made out anything of what had passed between them. 'Oh, it's OK,' she said without much conviction. 'Come on in for a cup of tea. It will be good to have a last chat with you before I go.'

Surprised, I entered the studio. Nothing could have been more of a contrast to its appearance on that day when I had gone to see where the spanner had been hidden. The entire place was completely bare, in every room, with the exception of one crate, about the size of a life-size sculpture.

'My competition piece for New York', Debbie explained. 'I had hoped that Max would let me use his van to take it to the airport, but he won't. I'm flying out with it tomorrow, and now I don't know what to do. There's no way I'm sending it by courier. Besides, I've already booked it as cargo.'

'Well,' I said, glad to find something mundane at the root of their argument. It didn't surprise me at all that Max wouldn't lend anyone anything, just at the moment! 'That van's not the only transport in the world. Let's have a cup of something, while I think of who else might be able to help you.' And indeed, after some thinking and a few phone calls, I had been able to arrange for a horse box to be lent for Debbie's sculpture, and even for a couple of helpers to load it. There were fork-lifts about the farm, and I was willing to get testy with Max if he had any objection to our borrowing one. The hay was in, and they were idle at the moment. Once at the airport, the people there would obviously be able to unload the crate and deal with it. Debbie began to relax, and even cheer up a bit.

As we sat drinking our tea, it struck me how forlorn the studio looked. 'But aren't you going to come back after the competition?' I asked her.

'Oh, of course, sooner or later. But I want to spend as much time as I can when I'm there, getting to know the market and making contacts. The Sculptors' Society has found me a room with another artist, that I can have for two months. I'm hoping that there'll be enough for me to accomplish to keep me there the whole time. If so, my husband will come out to join me for part of it. If worse comes to worse, I'll be back here in the autumn to start teaching again in the new term. But this could be my big break. I'm scared even to think about it, sometimes.'

'Well, everyone here will be keeping their fingers crossed for you. It will be sad for us if we lose you, but I wish you the very best of luck! Do remember us when you're famous,' I said, and she laughed happily, all the unpleasantness with Max forgotten.

16
The Parish Fête

The day of the parish *fête* dawned fair and warm, and no one was more excited than young Agrippa. From the time the curtains were opened in the morning he was glued to the front windows, his little tail a blur of wagging, watching people and things arrive. He was now nine months old, and convinced that life was a great, happy game staged for his own benefit. And now, as if in confirmation of that conviction, rather than having to continue his attempts to escape from the Rectory glebe to see the wider world, the world was coming to him! From time to time he was distracted from his observation post by wonderful smells emanating from the kitchen, as Angela prepared her fresh bread, rolls and cakes for the baked-goods stall. This would be the first public display of local crafts, culture, and produce for the visiting Italians, and Angela had reverted to type. Community, parish, and personal self-respect demanded an impressive show. She had been a little handicapped by not being able to bake the things she was best at: Irish *focaccia* and *pane rustico* would hardly do. On the other hand, she was not much taken with wheaten bread or fairy cakes. In the end she had invented a whole new range of breads and cakes using local produce, and was prepared to swear that they were *tipici*.

Finally she was ready to sally forth with the goodies, and an ecstatic puppy raced in circles about her feet as she made her way across the field to the church hall. In his progress Agrippa was able to inspect the tables being set up for the plant stall, the display of raffle items, the games, the horse boxes that had brought the ponies, and the huge mound of aluminium and nylon that would metamorphose miraculously into a marquee. It could be said that for an optimal account of the day's and evening's proceedings, Agrippa would certainly have been the best informant, could he but speak. Alone among all those who attended, he was very nearly everywhere at all times. In addition, he had the advantage of being such an innocuous presence that private conversation never failed, or was hushed, at his advent. Indeed the writer of the present narrative might well have wished that day not so much to have been a fly on a wall, as a puppy on the ground. Having deposited her offerings Angela returned to the house for her next task. She descended below stairs to the region she used for propagation and potting, and took stock of what she had prepared for the plant stall. All her cuttings were thriving, and many had grown into fledgling trees. Olives, figs, mulberries and vines, together with her herbs: bay, tarragon, basil and rosemary. She felt that these things, and these alone, would indicate to their guests that Ardliss was part of the civilised world. She only wished that she could grow nuts as well. But they would not be missed in the presence of her prize achievement: she had succeeded in raising some small orange and lemon trees in the green house, and looked forward to bearing them forth in triumph to put the finishing touch on the plant stall.

A small cart was of course needed to transport these sumptuous gifts, and more than one round trip; by the time everything was confided to the care of Rosie, the plant co-ordinator, her nursery was bare. Time now to raid the pantry. Jam and chutney making had never featured among Angela's culinary undertakings, but such was her anxiety to put on the best possible show that she had begged recipes from the parish's champion jam and pickle makers, and now had a respectable contribution to make to that cause. Loading her cart this time with jars, Angela noticed on crossing to the jam stall that long tables had been brought to one side of the field, where seasonal vegetables, fruit and honey were being set out. A vague uneasiness came over her. This *fête* would inevitably be different from the norm, and it had evolved in unusual ways. Strictly speaking vegetables, fruit and honey ought to have been reserved for the Ardliss agricultural display to be staged at the Abbey the following day. But of course, the parish was a great deal larger than just Ardliss, so that the *fête* was an opportunity for other towns, villages and townlands to get some benefit from the twinning. The day belonged as much to the two St Fechans as to All Saints Ardliss, and everyone in the parish was entitled to sell their produce in aid of its funds. If there was any entrepreneurial spin-off farther afield than Ardliss as a result, who could begrudge it? Besides, Angela herself was to some degree implicated in the phenomenon, in having decided to organise an art exhibition as part of the day's festivities. To be fair, she had not been thinking in terms of making sales, or finding new markets; it was rather her determination that the parish appear culturally respectable that had given her the idea. But then, one thing leading to another, it had transpired that the other artists in the parish had taken up the idea enthusiastically. 50% of sales was to be given to the parish. Angela was very grateful that on the whole the standard of amateur art locally wasn't too bad, since of course nothing could be turned down. She had personally contacted the better artists to ask for submissions, and had even wrested a few unsold pieces from Debbie before her departure. The exhibition thus stood a fair chance of making a very good appearance; and it would fill the otherwise redundant space in the marquee until the disco began. But then Eleanor Young of Greenborough had offered to sell some of her own-label designer clothes at 50% commission too, and in order to protect her things from possible rain they would also have to go into the marquee. This had threatened to make the exhibition look rather odd. In the end the best solution Angela had been able to think of was to bring out a couple of screens, and try to mark out a separate space for Eleanor.

On her way back from the jam stall, Angela started suddenly. Where was Agrippa? She looked about with alarm, fearing that he might have gone onto the road. But no, there he was! He had decided that the Italians who were setting up their wares in preparation for the barbecue were his new best friends. He was on a charm offensive, licking hands, and wiggling about, and rolling over on his back with his paws over his face. It seemed to be working, too, as usual! They had all stopped their work, and stood around admiring him, feeding him the odd tit-bit. As Angela walked over to rescue them, she noticed Louise driving her catering van up to the scene. 'Oh, who's doing the barbecue?' Angela asked her, having captured Agrippa.

'It's a compromise,' grinned Louise. 'They're doing wine, water, and samples of salami and cheese, and olive oil on bread. And you won't believe what I'm doing!'

'Go on,' said Angela, intrigued.

'Well, I've got *Mulcahy's* sausages and burgers, *Butler's* bacon and chops, and *Nippon Noodles* chow-mein with *Fishy Business* prawns and scallops. All donated, of course. Makes you queasy to think about, doesn't it? I'm hoping people will be sensible and not try to have some of everything!'

'That's rather irritating, isn't it?' said Angela. 'It's not really showing off Irish food. Besides, neither *Nippon Noodles* or *Fishy Business* are part of our parish!'

'Well, we're always grateful for donations, whoever makes them. Besides, I suppose *Nippon Noodles* counts as being in the parish, since Dickie Bird owned it.'

'*What*?' exclaimed Angela.

'Well, that's what I heard, anyway. When I went to collect the chow-mein ingredients from the warehouse, the manager said they were a bit worried about it. Dickie left no heirs, and apparently no will, so it's not clear who owns the business now.'

'What a mess,' said Angela, as much to herself as to Louise. Who now owned the rest of Dickie's business interests in the parish? And how many of them were there, exactly? 'I won't hold you up;' she continued as Louise set to work. 'I'd better put Agrippa inside to keep him away from the ponies.'

The noise and numbers of people and vehicles had increased significantly by the time Angela reached the house. It was now nearly 11:00 o'clock, and she had to start thinking about setting up the exhibition. Depositing a resistant Agrippa in his cage, she went to inspect the marquee, where Eleanor Young had already arrived with her van, loaded with clothes rails full of plastic-covered creations.

'Where do you think I should go?' asked Eleanor as Angela came up beside her.

'What about over here? You could have your own entrance.'

'Well,' said Eleanor doubtfully, 'I would really prefer not to look out at a lot of horses standing about making poohs.'

Angela didn't especially want that view for her exhibition either. 'Why on earth did they put one of the entrances facing the horse boxes?' she asked.

THE SERPENT IN THE GARDEN

'I don't suppose we can get them to turn the whole marquee for us,' said Eleanor wistfully.

'No, but I think you can change which sections are open or closed,' said Angela. 'Let's decide where we would each like our entrance, and then get them to open those sections for us.' The two of them went off in search of someone who could make the necessary adjustments.

There was a smell of lighter fluid as Louise perfected her charcoal, mingling strangely with that of candy-floss, as the first small customers assailed that van. A tinny tune heralded the arrival of an ice-cream seller. Balloons appeared in small hands, and some duly floated away. Plant and jam stalls were in readiness, and Bea had set out the raffle prizes and tombola, and was distributing books of tickets to her minions. The ponies were being warmed up for their customers, the games were nearly ready to play, the urns for tea were boiling, and the cakes and breads displayed to perfection. Stacks of gleaming rhubarb, carrots, potatoes, cauliflower, lettuces, spring onions and radishes were assembled for inspection, and there was an entire stall devoted to the various honeys of the parish. Eleanor positioned her screens and carefully removed plastic from her rails, and a troop of artists, under the generalship of Angela, deployed to hang the exhibition. There was the sound of mandolins tuning, and the popping of corks. With the inexorable momentum of such events the *fête* was about to reach critical mass and take off. Then, as if on cue, the Rector, identifiable to all in his white straw hat, strode to the car park to welcome Fr Enda and our local TD, who accompanied respectively the parish priest and mayor of Santa Maria degli Angeli. They descended from a white minibus which also held the rest of the Italian delegation. The crowds parted, the mandolins burst forth in greeting, *prosecco* and *antipasti* were served to the Irish committee, and *Guinness* to the Italians. Games began, ponies were mounted, raffle tickets were touted, burgers and chops sizzled, and chow-mein was prepared. The most memorable parish *fête* in living memory had begun.

Being as they were vastly outnumbered, the Italians were sitting targets for the Irish, and they were soon set upon from all sides by eager entrepreneurs. They were borne upon an enthusiastic eddy to the vegetable stall, the jam and pickle stall, and the honey stall. And it must be said that they bore the dazed expression of foreigners who have spent a week being fed Irish beef, lamb and pork, with Irish vegetables, Irish bread, butter, honey, jam and cake, washed down with Irish beer. At length they were swept into the church hall to be refreshed with Irish tea and to admire the cake stall. Here they were encouraged to sample creations made from local wheat, butter, honey and fruit. Then, as a respite before being regaled with Irish barbecue meat and chow-mein, they were encouraged to play games and inspect raffle prizes. At the plant stall their eyes hovered lovingly over the olives, figs and vines, familiar friends in this alien land. They would most likely have postponed with gratitude their cosmopolitan lunch, but for the fact that no one else could eat until they had.

THE SERPENT IN THE GARDEN

Graciously accepting a morsel of each of the featured products, they therefore took cover among the mandolins and fell upon the restorative virtues of wine and water.

In the midst of this exuberant *mêlée*, Claudia Crespi inhabited a world much like that of her beloved amphibians. Although a member of the Ardliss twinning committee, she was not part of the Church of Ireland parish, and thus counted as an Italian guest. She therefore took it upon herself to keep a watchful eye on the well-being of her countrymen. Once they were safely in the bosom of the *aperitivo*, therefore, she went in search of Angela to discuss where next to take them. It will not be a surprise that Angela strongly advised Claudia to bring them to the exhibition and fashion display, once they had sufficiently recovered. But here fate conspired against her. Once extracted from the *antipasti*, and on their way to the marquee, the delegation was distracted by the Pony Club, who had constructed a small jumping course (more for their own amusement than anything else). I had come over at Cathy's request to keep an eye on young Bobby, and couldn't help being rather amused at Angela's attempts to propel the delegation into the marquee. Lucy was standing not far away, eating burgers and sausages with a gusto that would have scandalised any Italian. I made my way over to her and said, 'I wonder whether you might like to go rescue your father?'

She looked over my shoulder and saw Steve being assailed by a small, gesticulating man. 'What's going on?' she asked.

'I have an idea that *Signor* Baffi — he's the mayor, you know — is enthusing about show jumping, and how much he admires it.'

Lucy's eyes widened. 'What's Dad said to him?'

'Nothing at all;' I replied. 'He is being a model of civility. But all the same . . .'

'I'm going!' she said, and shot off; for as we both knew, it was a question of rescuing *Signor* Baffi from Steve, rather than the other way round. I watched her draw the mayor away, and Steve came over to me.

'I thought he was going to drive me round the twist,' he said. 'If they're all like that, I don't know how I'm going get through tomorrow; but I've got to go really, for Lucy's sake.'

'Well, you can go to ground at my place for some of the time. The yard seems a bit quiet at the moment.'

'Oh, don't remind me of the yard. We've been hung out to dry by the probate people while they decide who owns Dickie's two now. We're getting basic expenses paid out of the estate, but we don't know what to do with them in the long run.'

'Do you mean to say,' I said, 'that Dickie actually owned, outright, two racehorses?'

Steve smiled at my surprise. 'Did you really not know how rich he was? I have an idea that he actually used that flat at the Abbey for lying low. He probably had houses and flats all over the place, and a passport to go with each one. That's what worries me about his horses. I reckon it will take years to sort out his estate, and decide who owns what. And I'm willing to wager it will end up belonging to the State. I can tell you, if I knew how I'd be sorely tempted to forge a will in my favour! Even once the dodgy bits are taken out, and death duties, anyone who inherited would be sitting very pretty. It wouldn't surprise me at all if once the dust settled some long-lost heir appeared from somewhere. Dickie would be just the sort to have secret wives and children scattered around the place.'

I must say that I was so taken aback by this that I was speechless. Steve's reasoning was faultless. Dickie always played a close hand, and I could well imagine him having amassed a tidy fortune without proclaiming it to the world. The same was true for personal relationships. Whatever ties Dickie had, it would have been just like him to form them abroad and keep them to himself. My mind turned to *Nippon Noodles*; for I too had heard that Dickie had registered the company. Had he a secret family in the Orient? Perhaps they had not yet heard of his death, but would produce a will once they had done so.

At this point Steve's attention was taken by a passing friend. We nodded goodbye, and I noticed that Angela had succeeded in capturing the Italian delegation for the exhibition. Not having seen the exhibition myself yet, let alone the designer fashions, I decided to follow them. But first I thought I ought to refresh myself with some *prosecco* and salami. The Italian wines were being scandalously neglected by most of the participants, and I reflected that it was one of the weaknesses of the impetus for twinning that each side was inclined to be more interested in showing off its own assets than in discovering those of its twin. There were far more Irish people drinking the Guinness, and Italians drinking their own local wine, than was strictly speaking to the point of the exercise. It therefore fell to those of us with more continental tastes to keep the side up. Accepting my glass, therefore, I paused to compliment the vintner, and was regaled with plates of salami and *bruschetta*, which I must say was dressed with the most wonderful oil. I began to encounter kindred spirits among the olives and smoked wild boar. Mark Charles was talking animatedly in Italian, and seemed to be enthusing about some artist or other. Mind you, my comprehension of Italian was at that time limited to those aspects that resemble Latin. Claudia was obviously taking time off from chaperoning the dignitaries, and was engaged in what was manifestly a business discussion with the *salumiere*. I was not surprised to observe that the Rector was with a party at a table nearby, which was liberally supplied with *antipasti*. He was at that moment in the act of bearing glasses and bottles of wine to a confraternity of clergy.

Replenishing my glass, I therefore made my way to the marquee and viewed the paintings. I was tempted by one of Angela's still lifes, a bowl of red pears; but where would I put it? Besides, having a professional artist in the parish rather spoils one, since it is possible to commission paintings at any time. I confess that I was curious as to what sort of fashions Eleanor designed, so I wandered into her area. I had read an interview with her in the *Irish Times*, but had never seen any of her clothes. 'So, you really don't think they would sell in Italy?' she was asking Angela. I must say that from what I saw, her dresses seemed rather on the whimsical side.

'They aren't sexy enough for the south,' said Angela with brutal honesty; 'and they aren't pared-down enough for the north. But you could certainly sell them in Tuscany. Give your line an Italian name, then sell them in any of the towns English-speaking tourists go to — which is almost all of them. You could make a fortune.'

At this point my interest in any mutual business benefits that might arise from the twinning was waning, and I was moreover becoming tired. Leaving the marquee I saw that the Rector was drawing numbers for the raffle. Agrippa had evidently been let out again, and was racing about begging for scraps and chewing discarded raffle tickets. The ponies were being prepared to go home. The mayor of Santa Maria degli Angeli won a lamb, and the parish priest won an evening dress; he took this in good part and said he was sure his sisters would quarrel over it. The exhibition was being dismantled, and the DJ's lorry had arrived and was parked by the hall, waiting to move in. The last cakes and buns were being sold half price, the final burgers were given away free, and the stalls were being dismantled. Cars were leaving, and the tired, happy throng dispersed either to recuperate in front of the television, or to take a deep breath before the disco. I gathered up my unsold plants and put them in the boot of the two-seater, peeled Theophrastes off the driver's seat, and went home. The *fête* was over. The official twinning festivities were yet to come.

17
Twinning Day

Needless to say, I was not among the revellers at the disco, though I was given to understand afterwards that it had been a great success. As is usual for such events, its reverberations were heard over a wide area, and those of us who anticipated an early start on Sunday were grateful when the volume was reduced at midnight. On returning home after the *fête* I had had a last liaison with Billy and Lucy about the races, and had fallen asleep that night running over in my mind any details we might have missed. I was therefore surprised, when I awoke to another clear, sunny morning, to discover that I myself had been infected with the excitement of the impending festivities. Even at that early hour, energetic preparations were in progress around the Abbey grounds. Bunting, balloons, and flags had been put in place the day before, and the gymkhana had been set up. But today the displays, especially those relating to food and horticulture, were being erected. *Bord Bia* was greatly in evidence, and the professional posters, leaflets, and computer presentations made a stark contrast to our homely efforts of the day before. There were also of course representatives promoting local tourism and heritage. I had never before seen so much of the County Council mobilised together at one time for one event. There was thus an excited buzz about the place, even though nothing was to begin until the afternoon. Angela and Claudia had pleaded the cause of our visitors, claiming that they were accustomed to having a decent nap after lunch. It had therefore been decided to restrict the entertainment at the official lunch, to allow time for a breather before everyone came on to the Abbey. The Irish dancing and traditional music were thus to form part of the afternoon's entertainment instead, which had the added advantage of allowing time to make them proper competitions, rather than simply short displays.

I had just enough time to check stable lines, water and hay, and inspect the starting line, before changing and heading off for church. Our service was of course not part of the official festivities, so it was nice to find that a few of the visitors had decided to come along to us rather than attending the official opening Mass, which was taking place at the same time. As they explained to us over coffee afterwards, we were of more cosmopolitan interest to them than watching their own parish priest concelebrate, and hearing a homily in English delivered by a Roman. I had a suspicion that Angela had paved the way for their appearance, making sure they all knew that they would be most welcome should they choose to join us. She had certainly seen to it that the church was beautifully decorated — as she said, 'just in case'. I must say that one of the benefits of the twinning exercise was that, in putting on a show for visitors, we were reminded of all the good and beautiful things of our own town and county. Roses and lavender, lilac and lilies, poppies, phlox and sidalcea; hemerocallis and chrysanthemums, eryngium and campanula, heliopsis and anemone; orchids in pots and foliage on boughs, filled the church with colour, and with a perfume as rich and magical as any incense. As I paused after coffee to adjust a couple of my own arrangements, I was complimented by one of our guests, an extremely elegant and well-turned-out young woman (*soignée*, as we would have said in my youth). As Angela and I left the church to make our way to Fr Enda's Community Centre, I asked who she was.

'Oh, *Signora* Falcone is a Communist politician,' she explained.

'Never!' I said in disbelief. 'How could any Communist wear such wonderful clothes and jewelry? I'm certain her necklace and bracelet are real gold.'

'Of course they are!' said Angela with a laugh. '*La bella figura*' is important to all Italians, even Communists!'

It seemed that I had much still to learn from our twinning venture!

I'm afraid that I dipped out of the official lunch after making a circuit with a glass of *prosecco*. A sandwich at home would have to do for me, and I'm afraid that Theophrastes suffered the indignity of a tin of cat food. Changing into jeans and wellies, and throwing a waxed hat and jacket on the back of the scooter just in case, I duly made my way down to the horses. Theophrastes always divines when I am about to do something equestrian, so I let him off by the door to the Great Hall, and he made his way at a leisurely pace around the Abbey, wending through the display stalls and tents, no doubt with the kitchen as his object. The Pony Club had set up their gymkhana in the field in front of the Great Hall, but I was making for the racing lines on the other side of the house.

While setting Theophrastes down I became increasingly aware of the escalation in activity that had taken place since I had ventured out in the morning. The car park was thronged with cars and vans, and horseboxes lined the road beside the gymkhana venue. These were gradually moving off to park outside the park at the back, on the wide verge leading to the forest track; but it was all rather a muddle in the meantime. Some of the van men who had brought displays and such like were now packing their empty crates and boxes back into their vehicles and moving them out of the park. Extra estate workers had been hired as traffic and parking wardens, as is usual for big events at the Abbey. Likewise, the parking area immediately in front of the Great Hall (though accessible to me by scooter), was cordoned off as reserved parking for guests and dignitaries. In the same way, the inner courtyard, by the back door of the Abbey, was a mass of vehicles and activity. Louise's catering van was there, along with *Fishy Business*, and most of our local food producers.

As I steered my way through the throng, around to the ornamental gardens, I made a detour to see how Cathy was getting on. Her borders were magnificent, and the summer fruiting trees were breathtaking. I looked in at the walled market garden, and saw a couple of gardeners standing, as proud as sentries awaiting official inspection. I called to them to ask where Cathy was, and they directed me to the llama enclosure. There I found her, standing next to the now infamous compost digester, looking suspiciously at the camelids.

'I have a terrible feeling that some horrid child is going to let them out, just for fun,' Cathy said when she saw me. 'Do you remember what happened in the vegetable garden the last time they got out? It doesn't bear thinking about.'

'I'm surprised Helena hasn't thought of that already,' I replied. 'She's generally very careful of them, especially after that awful incident with the toffee apple.'

'Oh I've no doubt that she's taken every precaution for their protection; hence the new screening. I'm more concerned about protecting the garden *from* them.'

'Wouldn't a good sturdy lock do? The fencing should be child-proof otherwise,' I suggested.

'That's just what I said to Billy, and the dear fellow has gone off to find one for me. He really has been invaluable to everyone lately.'

'Don't I know it!' I agreed. 'So are you just standing guard until he arrives back?'

'Something like that,' said Cathy smiling. 'I suppose that mostly I'm trying to keep out of the way. There's nothing more we can do now in the garden without spoiling it, and now I just wish the whole day was over. They're not just being shown the gardens, they'll also have to go through them on their tour of the ponds, so I won't be off duty until they return from that.'

'I promise to come and keep you company after the races,' I said. 'I'll raid the produce displays and bring us a picnic.'

'That would be nice,' she replied, perking up. 'But aren't you entertaining any of the racing lot?'

'No, no. The hunt has got its own catering arranged. I'm turning my flat over to Alice and Lucy so they can change and have a rest after the races, so I'll want to stay out of their way. Alice has to stay on to supervise the Pony Club barbecue this evening. Did you know that Lucy has been asked to drinks and dinner? I was so pleased, and I think even Steve was, though he wouldn't want to admit it. She's done so much, it's good to see her get some recognition.'

'No, I hadn't heard! That is good news. All right then, bring us a picnic, and we can have a rest before cleaning up and changing for drinks,' Cathy said. 'I have to admit that I'm relieved not to be on the guest list for dinner. I'm going to feel all in. Are you going?'

'Hardly!' I said. 'I've done my best to do as little as possible for all this, as you know. No, I've asked Steve to come back later and have a bite with me, so Lucy can enjoy herself at the dinner, and he can drive her home after the fireworks. What were you going to do for dinner? Why don't you join us, if you've nothing else planned?'

'No, no,' Cathy replied hastily. 'I've got a nice quiche in, and I'm going to fill the bath with bubbles, open some champagne, put on some Verdi, and luxuriate.'

'Well done!' I said. 'I'd better push on now and get sorted for my show. I'll see you soon with whatever goodies I can scrounge. I'll just give you a tip off by phone, shall I?'

'Yes, do!' she replied, adding somewhat prophetically, 'Whatever would we do without our wonderful little phones?'

Continuing around towards the back of the house, I dismounted to lead my scooter down the stairs and the pool path, to the fields where the races would commence. The public rooms of the Abbey — library, dining room, etc — have large windows giving onto a wide terrace at the back of the house. In front of the terrace is a small lawn, and beyond that the ground slopes steeply down to fields and meadows, making a spectacular view to the north. Standing on the terrace or lawn one sees not only arable and grazing land. To one's right, running like a tongue between fields, a plantation of trees leading down from the ornamental and vegetable gardens marks the course of the stream, and its famous pools. It had therefore been decided that the races would begin and end in the field nearest the lawn, so that guests would have a panoramic view, with most of the course in sight. The terrace was to be devoted to the Irish dancing, so that everywhere one wandered there would be something of interest. Commercial displays and gymkhana in front of the main entrance, traditional music in the tea room, dancing on the terrace, and races in the fields beyond. The dignitaries were to be taken by

William personally on a tour of the ponds. After a short break, the harp and organ concert would take place in the Great Hall, followed by speeches. A drinks reception would then be held in the library for guests, dignitaries, committee members, and those who had worked especially hard on the preparations. A formal dinner would conclude the festivities, culminating in the fireworks display.

As I made my way down through the gardens to the field below, I therefore congratulated myself that my responsibilities were as limited as they were. The hunt had done most of the work in setting up the races, so I had been able to concentrate on the starting and finishing. There were plenty of volunteers for stewarding, and Steve had pitched in, offering to call and inspect starters. Ironically, the 'gnats' had probably caused more work than any of the other races! For steeplechases, you're either over or you're not, but a flat course across country takes a lot of diligence to make sure everyone goes round properly. Bobby Baskerville was favourite to win, young as he was; he was certainly on the most powerful pony. We had decided to give the gnats a thrill and weigh them like proper jockeys, so that was yet more work.

Arriving down at the lines I found that many others had skipped lunch (and in some cases church, I am sorry to say), and were well ahead of me. Lucy was to oversee gnats and maidens, but would hand over to others for the hunter chases, enabling her to have some fun herself. Dirty Flirty was looking good in Alice's class, and Lucy would have a good chance on Sapphire in hers. So it was nice that Steve had taken time to come and help. Work at the yard continued apace, twinning or no twinning, so he was to head back as soon as the last race finished, taking Sapphire with him. As I pulled up and parked where we had established our lines, I was surprised to see that the field wasn't littered with horseboxes. 'Where are the boxes?' I asked Lucy as I joined her.

'Over beyond the ponds, on that lane that forks off the forest road,' she replied.

This I could make no sense of. 'Don't you mean the avenue?' I asked. 'I assumed that they had been left there, and the horses ridden over. But there's not enough of a verge, so I wondered how guests could arrive if trailers were left on the drive.'

'No, no,' Lucy replied emphatically. 'Everyone came up through the forest, off the Rathcoole road. Helena thought it would be less of an eyesore, which is probably right. But it's meant everyone having to ride across, and carry all their kit, which is a bit of a nuisance.'

'Quite,' I said. 'But what I mean to say is, how did they *get* to the other side of the stream, through the forest? Surely nothing as big as a horsebox could get up the forest track.'

'Oh!' she said, surprised. 'I assumed you'd know all about it. Max kept agitating to have access direct to the farm from the Rathcoole road, through the forest. William finally agreed, so now they've got the whole track widened and levelled, and gravel down, all the way to the end of the estate, so you can come straight here off the Rathcoole road without going into Ardliss at all. It's been up and going for a couple of weeks. That's how I brought our novices up from our yard.'

I must admit that I felt rather embarrassed. By dipping out of so much lately, I had completely missed this development, literally on my doorstep. To change the subject I asked Lucy (since she seemed to know all about the estate now!) — 'Who on earth are the people prowling around in the trees, do you know? There were more in front of the house as well. They look rather dubious to me.'

'Go and tell them that!' she answered, amused. 'They're Guards!'

'Oh no! What's happened now?'

'Nothing, as far as I know, and that's the way they want it to stay. I'm told these are special detectives, bodyguards for the ambassadors and politicians. We had to have words with them this morning, because they were messing around the jumps, and poking in the hedges. Dad told them straight out, "If you're still at that when the racing starts, you'll either get yourselves killed, or worse." One of them was cheeky and asked, What could be worse than getting killed, so of course Dad said, 'Getting one of our horses or riders killed!'

I sighed. Perhaps I would have been better to miss church myself, to keep an eye on Steve! But whatever his exchanges with the personal protection people had been, it seemed to have been effective. They kept off our course, and from my point of view, things couldn't have proceeded better. In due course we heard the band playing, and it was evident that the dignitaries were arriving. We were working to our own timetable, and it was up to them to watch the races or not, so it was some time before any of us were able to pay much attention to what was happening up above. Our first concern was to assemble and weigh gnats, see them up and brought forward, and off. We had the satisfaction of seeing a few startled plain-clothes men pop up on the lawn above when I fired the start! I have to say that the gnats gave good value for the effort we had put into them. It's amazing what monkeys children of that age are. Little Siobhan Gallagher skidded at a sharp turn, and we all assumed she was down; but she was glued to her pony, which righted itself, and she was still in the middle of the field even after the fall. Bobby Baskerville obviously considered it to be his destiny to win, and the others as obviously thought it theirs to wipe his eye. As competitive sport, it was rivetting. Coming round the last corner Bobby was neck and neck with Jason Kelly, but neither of them saw Rachel Murphy, straddled across Sunbeam's neck, pulling away from the field behind them. Inexorably she drew up to the leaders, but as in the most exciting races, the question was whether she had left it too late. They were three abreast coming to the finish, and we were praying that it would be a clear win. Just at the line, they came in cleanly, Sunbeam by a neck, then Bobby on Wrecker beating Jason on Batman by a head. It was easily the most exciting finish of the day.

After the gnats, everything else went like clockwork. Alice floated around, and Flirty finished two lengths ahead of the field. There were falls in Lucy's class, so she finished way out in front. Steve was obviously pleased and proud, but we all knew that there would be more trouble to come with Alice over getting a licence. With the races finished, it took everyone a while to dismantle and pack up, but Steve was quickly away to get back to work. I found myself blissfully redundant, and went back to the flat to clean up and change before handing it over to the girls. With the euphoria of a job well done, I drifted through the Abbey kitchen as boldly as Theophrastes himself, acquiring from Penny the makings of a first rate picnic. This, together with a bottle of *prosecco* and another of mineral water, I bore in triumph to Cathy, and we had a very pleasant meal, upwind of the llamas.

When I returned to the flat it was getting on. The girls were changed and at the concert. Cathy was going to have a rest before bathing and changing for drinks, and I thought it a good idea to do the same. Heaven only knows where Theophrastes was, but that was his affair. I woke just in time to change, and made my way over to Cathy's, and we headed to the library together along the internal corridor. A dozen or so other guests were there ahead of us. It was now a wonderful evening, the sort of midsummer we always think we remember, but seldom experience: cloudless and clear, the low sun casting long shadows and the early stars blazing. There was a fire in the hearth for atmosphere more than warmth, and the windows were open to the harpists on the terrace. The first earl gazed proudly from his frame. 'What a perfect evening,' Cathy said to me. 'What a perfect day! Do you know, they actually noticed the gardens! Of course, Italians are famous for gardens, and it made me so proud that they were impressed with ours.'

'Yes, I'd say we've all done our jobs well,' I answered. 'Now for a pleasant evening, and fireworks at the end.'

Not long after our arrival, Lucy came in through the terrace. She was looking lovely in a simple silver gown. I could tell from her smile and sparkling eyes that her sentiments were the same as ours! 'Well done!' we said to her, and I handed her a glass of *prosecco*. 'You've done a great job,' I said, 'and now I hope you can enjoy the evening!'

'I can't believe it all went off so well! Even my novices did well. I think Dad was pleased too. He's said to remind you that he'll be back with you for dinner, and then he can take both of us and Flirty back.'

'Oh,' said Cathy. 'Will Alice be sharing the barbecue with the Pony Club?'

'Oh, yes; that's the reward for trying to look after them!' Lucy answered.

'Oh, that's alright then,' said Cathy. 'You should be having a really first-rate dinner with the VIPs. Every sort of local provision and delicacy seems to have been brought in for the occasion!'

'Yes, I'd say so from what I saw in the courtyard coming over here. I found Agrippa sniffing rapturously around the food vans. He was dying to get into the *Fishy Business* van! He was so agitated that I actually opened it to see what he was on about. You know, it was curious, because when I looked into the back of the van I saw—'

BANG! At first I thought it was my starting pistol. But there was a shatter as Lucy's glass hit the floor before the fire, *prosecco* bubbling from it. She fell slowly onto the carpet, and on the silver of her dress there grew a crimson stain, as bright as the curtains behind the first earl.

18
The Chase

A dozen things happened at once. Suddenly, the whole world seemed to go into slow motion, so that I was able to observe things in detail, and without a feeling of being rushed, even though in reality very little time elapsed. I had heard of this phenomenon, but it was the first time that I had experienced it for myself. Two of the cocktail guests were kneeling beside Lucy and attending to her. I recognised one of them as a distinguished surgeon, so she was obviously in good hands. The other attendant was reaching for his mobile phone, presumably to call an ambulance. The harpists on the terrace were screaming, and several bodyguards were running in through the terrace windows. Probably less than a minute had elapsed when I turned to Cathy and said, calmly but with urgency, 'Turn your phone on so I can contact you.' She had just time to nod before I was away, running through the Great Hall with that same leisurely sensation, and through the main doors. If the assailant had fled across the terrace, plain clothes police would be after him. If he was still in the house, they would find him. But with the corner of my eye I had caught a movement, which although I couldn't analyse it rationally, I associated with the door in the panelling, beside the fireplace in the library.

It was obvious that none of the guests in the Hall had heard anything, nor the people packing their demonstrations in front. I was aware of people turning and staring at me; I must have made a strange sight pelting along in evening dress. The fires from the Pony Club barbecue were in front of me, and I saw that the children had obviously been hacking in the park — most of the ponies were still out, and saddled. Alice stood up and looked at me, and somehow I must have made some telepathic communication with her, because she started running towards me. I sprinted over the cattle grid towards the courtyard entrance.

I was just approaching the courtyard gate when there was a squealing and grinding noise, and a white van shot out. Blazoned across the side I read a familiar device: *Fishy Business*. The insufferable cheek of it! The chancer had been taunting us all the time. As he turned sharply right to get to the drive, he nearly collided with Steve's car, coming down the hill to keep our appointment. Swerving onto the grass he got round the car, as Steve screeched to a halt. By now people were becoming aware that there was something amiss. Alice was running towards her father's car, and Bobby Baskerville, always in the midst of everything, was with her. We converged on Steve together, and I said as quickly as I could, 'After that van; he's shot Lucy.'

Steve's eyes widened, but he spoke not a word, simply turning his car as quickly as he could. I turned to the two children, whose pale faces looked at me in disbelief. 'You two go point,' I said as I opened the passenger door and got in. 'We must know which way he turns when he reaches the road! Bobby, cut across the fields towards the Rectory. You should have a view of the road. Alice, you'll have to take the park wall and get to high ground in case he's making for Drum. Put your phones on so I can call you!' I shouted after them as they tightened girths and let down stirrups.

'Who is this bastard, and why did should he shoot my girl?' asked Steve once I was in and we were off.

'I've no idea,' I confessed. 'But he knows the house, and the grounds, and I suspect the whole country.' I was establishing a conference call with Alice, Bobby and Cathy, as quickly as I could manage. Thankfully I had the numbers of all the jockeys from the races, even the gnats. I saw Alice speed past us, and carry on west as we turned into the drive. I would wait to call her until I was certain that she was over the wall. 'It's just come back to me,' I said as we collided with speed ramps down the drive, 'that Lucy was just about to tell us something about that van when she was shot. She had seen something in the back, but just when she was going to tell us —'

Looking to my right I saw Bobby cutting diagonally across the fields towards the Rectory, followed by several of the other children.

'He's heading for Drum!' came Alice's voice, just in time for us to turn onto the road without dithering. 'He could turn off anywhere, so I'll keep an eye on him from the high ground.'

'Bobby, you're to come straight back to the Abbey now,' said Cathy's voice. 'Tell Steve that Lucy's not dead, Robbie. They're getting an ambulance, and there were paramedics on standby here in any case.'

'Why do I have to come back? I could cut across the field by the school and —'

'Bobby, you're to come straight back this minute, or you'll be grounded from hunting for the whole season. I mean it.'

'Oh, Gran —'

'The Guards are here, and they want to interview you,' feinted Cathy. This must have done the trick, because we were mercifully spared any more of Bobby.

'Cathy,' I said, 'tell the Guards that he's in a —'

'Yes, yes, I've got all that. I'll keep feeding them Alice's news.'

Suddenly, a couple of hundred yards ahead of us, Alice appeared over the hedge to our left, onto the road, and over the opposite hedge. I thought Steve would have a fit, but he simply said, 'He's turned off to the north.'

'He's on the Old Road,' came Alice's voice, now that she could free a hand for the phone.

'Well, at least we know that he has to appear at the other end. If he tries anything else, we'll get him,' I said.

'Robbie, I'm in a Garda car. Can you give us any idea where to go?' came Cathy's voice.

I was just about to say that we only knew that he would emerge onto the bog road, when inspiration struck me, rather belatedly. 'Noyestown,' I said. 'Not the village, the road leading to it from the bog road.' And sure enough, having spent what seemed an eternity weaving along the Old Road, we emerged onto the bog and caught sight of the van speeding off west. Once on the road, we were able to gain some ground on it. We were close enough to see him turn up towards Noyestown, and when we reached the turning, there was Alice on the verge waiting for us, pointing after him. There was no longer any farmland for her to ride over, and she had already overdone Flirty on the tarmac of the bog road. As we waved to her she gave us a nod, and turned to trot away home on what little of the verge there was by the road. 'She's a great girl, Steve,' I said, looking back at her confident figure retreating from us.

'Both my girls are first rate,' he replied grimly.

'We're not far behind you, Robbie,' came Cathy's voice. 'We just made you out at the turning towards Noyestown. They've got another car too, coming across from the Greenborough road.'

'They'll be too late,' I said. 'He's headed for the lake, down the road by the noodle warehouse. I can't think of any other way to get there except from here or Noyestown.'

'OK,' said Cathy, and I heard her conferring with the Guards.

'How do you know where he's going?' asked Steve.

'Oh, just pasting rumours together,' I said.

The van was making good speed, but Steve's four by four was more powerful, and we were gaining on him. But it seemed a hopeless aspiration to think that we could catch him before he got to the lake. And if he was aware that we were expecting that, he might well decide to carry on to Noyestown, where he would have his choice of roads to follow, and it would be easy to lose us. But then, suddenly, just as it was beginning to look hopeless, we were aware of something on the road ahead of him. A tractor, heaven be praised!, coming off the bog and turning slowly in front of the van. The quarry accelerated, hoping to cut round the tractor before it was quite on the road. But he clipped it and spun onto the narrow verge, then toppled sideways into a cutting. The tractor driver had stopped, and was looking back aghast. 'He's crashed!' I said to Cathy. 'Do tell them to hurry; he's probably still got the gun.'

'We can see you! They say to stay in your car and not to approach him.' But before I could stop him, Steve was out like an avenging angel. He dashed over to the van, jerked open the passenger door (which was uppermost), and hauled the occupant out by main force. I was dashing up behind, encumbered by my dress shoes, when he got the fellow onto the ground and turned him over. As I leant over his shoulder, we both gasped.

'*Mr Moto*!' I cried. The Guards had arrived, and were pounding up behind us. They were just in time to prevent Steve throttling him. As they pulled Steve away, Cathy came up, and between us we got him to come back to the car and sit down.

'He's killed my little girl', he said, in a numb agony.

'No, no,' said Cathy, soothingly. 'She'll be alright. She's in good hands. Let's get you back, and you can talk to the doctors yourself.'

'But he *wanted* to kill her. Why would anyone want to kill her?'

And as if in answer, two of the Guards moved round and opened the back of the van. Despite ourselves, we all three went over behind them to see what on earth Lucy had seen that could have given rise to being shot at. And there, in all its baffling incongruity, was a silage bag. One of the detectives was muttering expletives. As they moved to inspect the bag, a rat jumped out of the van: presumably the source of Agrippa's previous agitation. As the Guards fell back in consternation, I took the opportunity to move up and step into the back of the van. And there on the silage bag's side, as if in mockery of us, I saw a large white smiley face.

'You make me crash! You steal silage!' By now Mr Moto was upright, and seizing the opportunity of the detectives' confusion. But all the pieces of the puzzle had now fallen into place in my mind. All those years of following the various arguments associated with the Christological controversies had left me with a finely honed feeling for the relationships between pieces of evidence, and this was now bearing unexpectedly pragmatic fruit.

'I think you'll find stolen antiquities from the Abbey in that bag,' I said, with an authority that surprised everyone, including me. 'They will probably have been packed in straw. He was on his way to meet his accomplice before fleeing. You must hurry before he escapes! Moto has doubtless already warned him. Hurry!' I nearly had to drag one of the detectives into his car, but at last I got him to understand, and we sped off towards Noyestown, as I explained as succinctly as I could. Once he saw the urgency, I had no cause to complain of a deficiency in speed! He communicated with his colleagues, but I'm afraid that I was too absorbed in the chase to update Cathy, even though I had left her standing with Steve, both of them in a state of bewildered incomprehension. We reached the noodle warehouse just as the 'manager' was trying to close the doors on us. But the detective was able to rush the car in before he got the doors across, making the fellow leap out of the way. Other Garda cars were following us, as we skidded to a halt behind a Nippon Noodles lorry, fitted with a ramp and obviously prepared to receive the fish van. What a fool I had been! The truth had been staring me in the face all along. How could I have thought that any self-respecting Chinese would have given his business a Japanese name?

The *soi disant* noodle distributor was putting up an indignant show, but my explanation to the detective had obviously been coherent, because he immediately instructed the others to seize the ferry belonging to the Meditation Centre, and make for the island. I, of course, did not follow. I had deduced well enough what they would find. Feeling suddenly cold and shaky, I rang Cathy, only to find that she and Steve had followed the

Garda cars, and were waiting outside. It was with gratitude that I found them, and they put me in the car and brought me home. By this time I was shivering.

'We need to get some brandy into you, and then something to eat,' said Cathy, who sat beside me as Steve drove.

'How's Lucy?' I asked.

'They've taken her to Dublin,' she replied; 'she's not great, but she doesn't look like expiring just yet.'

And so we made our way back to the Abbey, found Alice, and got back to my flat, where Cathy and Steve, despite his trauma, sat me down and fed and watered me. Once I had some brandy I came round a bit, and their curiosity gained the upper hand.

'What on earth has been going on, Robbie?' asked Steve. 'You seem to know all about it.'

'I have understood nothing, up to the time that I saw Moto and that silage bag. And now I could curse myself for a fool for not having seen it all before. He's been stealing things, from the Abbey; I don't know what, and I don't know why. But he's been stashing them in silage bags, which he's been transporting via the fish van to the noodle warehouse. Whatever he's been taking has left packing materials, or something, that he's been dumping on the bog at night. The noodle lorry has then been taking the goods somewhere to dispose of them; I assume either a 'fence' (if that is still the correct term), or a ship or airplane.'

'But where does the Meditation Centre come in?' asked Steve.

'I have no doubt that, when they arrive on that island, they will discover a helicopter, in readiness for their escape. This was to be the last load. Moto has been telling us that he would be moving on to the Continent, but my suspicion is that he would never have been heard of again.'

'But how can you possibly be sure of all this?' asked Cathy, quite justifiably.

'Because it accounts for all the evidence. Michael Slattery was either involved, or discovered something. Dickie, I'm afraid, probably came to grief through playing a lone hand. The only things I don't pretend to understand are, exactly what he was stealing, why, and how he intended to dispose of it.'

By this time, I confess that I was tiring. There was nothing more we could do until the Guards revealed what they discovered. I made Steve and Alice eat something before they returned home; I knew that they would have a long night driving to Dublin and back. Cathy sat with me for a while, and I have to say that even Theophrastes seemed to look at me with a newfound respect. At length I went to bed, and fell into a fitful sleep, wondering what revelations the morning would bring.

19
Revelations

To my great vexation, very little more came to light the next day, or indeed the next week. Beyond the fact that a helicopter had indeed been found on the island, the Guards were determinedly uncommunicative. There were conferences *in camera* with William and Helena, but no one was willing to give me the least idea of what was happening. This I'm afraid I regarded as rather ungrateful on the part of the Guards, given that I had made possible the capture of the warehouse accomplice and the discovery of the helicopter. When I saw my detective again and put this to him, he had the audacity to say that they would have found them in any case! I had thought that we had established a fraternal bond during the chase, but seemingly this was not the case. I became resigned to learning everything through reports of the trial, whenever that was to be. In the meantime, I had no option but to return to as normal a life as was possible, given the circumstances. Cathy quite sensibly encouraged me to be satisfied that the murderer was now caught; the important thing was that we were all safe now. And this was of course true. Lucy would spend some time in hospital, but she was soon out of danger. Our next fear was that she would be left with permanent injuries that would impair her health in the long run. But we were gradually reassured on that front too.

J.E. RUTHERFORD

For want of any other diversion, I raided my piggy bank and traded my antique sports car for a new, state of the art model. The new academic year was fast approaching, and I would have to adjust myself to returning to the old commute after a respite of three years. In the meantime it made travelling to see Lucy much more comfortable for Cathy and me. We amused ourselves learning how to raise and lower the top with the press of a button. But it took us a while to learn what all the other controls and indicators meant, and I still haven't become used to the car talking to me (I am tempted to say 'nagging me'). It was disconcerting to find that when I turn my phone on inside the car, it automatically links up to the car radio, and even recognises the phone's address book. But this was only an extension of our previous excursions into microtechnology, and we persevered, seeing how useful this would ultimately be. What with visiting Lucy, and helping Steve at the yard, and checking proofs of my new *magnum opus*, the unresolved mystery sank to the back of my mind. It was therefore with a stoical resignation that I went about my daily routine.

Then one day, going to the vegetable garden in search of Cathy, I found Helena inspecting the lettuces, with an eagle eye out for slugs. 'Hello,' I ventured; 'I assume that all's well with the ponds, if you're able to turn your attention to vegetables for a while.'

'Oh, hello Robbie,' she replied. 'Yes, fortunately William had to stay at home longer than he had anticipated, to deal with the aftermath of Mr Moto. He was therefore able to see to them himself for a change, and everything's settled down, I'm happy to say. You must get down before you miss the best of the flowers and butterflies; the dragonflies and salamanders are very handsome, too; frogs and newts I'm afraid I can only regard as quaint.'

'Yes, I'm afraid that I've neglected the ponds sadly, what with one thing and another,' I said.

'Well, of course!' said Helena. 'I understand that Lucy Blackmore is coming along well. It's so nice that you have the new car now for getting up and down. How long does it take you?'

'About an hour now, with that new stretch of motorway,' I replied. 'So are you finally rid of the police?' I ventured, tactfully as I thought.

'Oh, if only!' she said with a groan. 'It looks like going on for years. If things go on like this, we'll have to give Mark Charles a long lease so that he can make the house his life's work. Of course you will have heard all about it.'

'Oh, quite;' I said, with what I intended as heavy sarcasm. 'The Guards regard me as an indispensable collaborator.'

'That's what I thought,' said Helena innocently, having missed my tone. 'It makes it so much more bearable for me, having someone at the Abbey with whom I can speak freely about the whole mess while it's still *sub judice*.'

Now this was fortuitous, and I'm afraid that I didn't rush to disabuse her of her misapprehension. I followed as Helena moved out through the garden gate and sat on a bench overlooking the woods where the ponds lay. Taking my courage in my hands, I decided on an opening gambit. 'I'm afraid that I don't yet understand the extent of the thefts,' I said.

'Well, no, how could you?' Helena replied. 'Being informed is one thing, being a mind reader is another. Of course he's not admitting any of the thefts except what the police find; that's why Mark Charles is having to start his catalogue all over again.'

'It's a pity Mark didn't cotton on to things himself,' I suggested, daring a little more.

'Oh, Robbie, not you too!' Helena said with disapproval. 'The Guards are still inclined to suspect him of being involved, even though it's obvious that Mr Moto was following after him, substituting replicas of things Mark had already catalogued. They have even got him to admit that it was Mark's presence that decided him to move his operations here. He regarded Mark as the perfect cover for his thefts, since Mark's catalogue would effectively guarantee the genuineness of the articles.'

Emboldened by the success of my surmises thus far, I made another gamble. 'But surely it was Dickie who told him about the Abbey.'

'Of course; he had met Dickie in Japan before, and Dickie had told him about Mark being here. They planned it together, I'm sorry to say.'

'Poor Dickie,' I said, growing ever more confident. 'He always did play a lone hand. His speculations with the field and the lake drew attention to him, and that had already annoyed Moto, before Dickie's fatal mistake of trying to swindle Wendy Noyes out of her watercolours. That could have ruined the whole operation, and landed them both in prison. At that point, Dickie became expendable. What I don't understand,' I said, considering that I had established enough credibility to confess a little ignorance, 'is what Michael Slattery did to get himself killed.'

'No, I haven't heard any more on that front, either,' said Helena to my great satisfaction. 'All Mr Moto will say is that Michael snooped into everything, and was very irritating. It sounds very much like curiosity killing the cat.'

'Yes,' I mused; 'Michael probably saw himself like that, subtle and feline. In reality he was enormously transparent.'

'And he quite evidently did not have nine lives,' observed Helena.

I was doing so well, that I decided to push my luck a little further. 'Of course, Dickie wasn't really useful to Moto once he had set up Nippon Noodles and the Meditation Centre in his own name.'

'Well, I daresay he was *useful*, but not essential,' replied Helena. 'Technically, his signature was required on the export licences needed for sending the things back to Japan; but it would have been easy for them to have forged that. I don't understand, though, why no one thought it suspicious that a Japanese food supplier was registered as both an import and an export concern. But then I don't really understand business.'

'No;' I said. 'No more do I. But of course, Dickie did, poor chap.'

I could think of only one more gambit, and could only hope that it would elicit the maximum remaining information. 'What about that place it was all going to?' I asked, fearing that this betrayed a suspicious degree of ignorance. But I needn't have worried.

'Oh, the English Big House Wedding Heaven?' Helena replied. 'It's extraordinary, isn't it; imagine Japanese Shintoists wanting western style white weddings.'

Well, this was something I must confess that I had never suspected! Before I could stop myself, I exclaimed, '*English*! He might have had the decency to say *Irish* Big House Wedding Heaven!'

'Well, quite!' said Helena, 'To be honest, we felt that as more of an affront than the thefts! But once we learned that the wedding resort contains a Scottish baronial castle, a Welsh Methodist chapel, and a Cotswold Cottage (supposedly the home of Beatrix Potter's aunt), we felt that we were only one of many victims.'

I was digesting these facts as quickly as if I were attending a very important academic conference. 'Of course,' I said, 'a Calvinist Methodist chapel would suit them better than any other sort of church, because it's obviously western, but devoid of overt religious images.'

'Oh! Do you know, the Guards hadn't thought of that. I must mention it when I see them later today,' said Helena. 'Unless you'd rather tell them yourself.'

'No, no,' I hastily demurred. 'You'll see them before I do. Besides, I don't suppose it's of more than theoretical interest. When will you start receiving your things back?' I asked, to change the subject.

'Oh, don't depress me. The longer it takes, the better.'

'What?' I asked, confused.

'All the reproductions are so beautifully made; and the organ works! Why should I want those old rotten things back? I only wish he had finished all the chapel panelling before he was caught.'

It took me a minute to digest this. 'Of course, he would only have wanted the organ case; I dare say it was the internal workings that they were dumping on Christmas Eve.'

'Exactly. He intended it to have electronic workings once it was installed in his resort.'

At this point, my curiosity was pretty much satisfied, and I must say that I was rather pleased with my deductions so far. It was therefore more for conversation than to elicit information that I said, 'It's extraordinary, isn't it. It's hard to imagine that good quality reproductions would be considered of less value than scruffy originals. That organ must have been very expensive to copy.'

'I know!' agreed Helena. 'I'm told though that because the Japanese are such experts at reproduction, it isn't valued very highly. Whereas real, genuinely old, wormy things are hugely admired. That's what gives the English Big House Wedding Heaven its *cachet*, I understand. If only he had got round to taking the roof.'

'Was that what he was investigating when he dropped the virtual pet in the roof-space?' I asked, with another sudden burst of illumination.

'No, he was just poking around to see if we had any old junk stored up there. The great mercy, though, is that Mark thought to have the paintings cleaned. Did they tell you, he would have stolen them if they had still been dirty and yellow? But once they were cleaned they looked too new!'

'Aren't cultural differences extraordinary?' I asked. I confess that I experienced a high degree of satisfaction over the accuracy of my surmises.

'Yes;' Helena concurred. 'I suppose it's true that "East is east and west is west", as I believe Annie Oakley once observed.'

And so it was that I was able to return to my own affairs with the satisfaction of knowing that my reconstruction of events had been substantially accurate. I had also the satisfaction of having discovered details of which I had been ignorant. It is true that I hadn't the satisfaction of being credited with my deductions, but as a scholar, that was nothing new.

It was therefore with my mind on my own concerns that I set out with Cathy about a week later for a leisurely walk. Meandering along the pond path, we came across Mark staring sightlessly among the dragonflies, down into the depths between the lily pads, looking rather like a disappointed Narcissus. 'What's the matter, Mark?' asked Cathy. 'Surely everything is sorted out now, and no one can suspect you of anything any more.'

'You have no idea at *all*,' he replied, without taking his eyes from the water. 'My professional reputation will never recover from this.'

'What on earth do you mean?' said Cathy. 'You have been proven to be absolutely unconnected with anything criminal, and that will surely come out during the trial.'

Turning to look at us with haggard eyed, he said, 'Yes, and that's what's most damnable.'

'What do you mean?'

'Here I was, actually in the process of cataloguing the very things that were stolen and faked, right from under my nose. I will never recover from this. I'll be a laughing stock. It would have been much better for me to have actually been one of the gang.'

'Mark!' I said, aghast.

'Well, it would. I don't know what to do. I'm afraid to think what will happen when I go back to consultancy. I can't hope for any more work from the big auction houses. What's the point of expecting to work again at all? When all this comes out it will look as if I can't even spot reproductions.'

'Now, steady on and get a grip,' I said. 'It is bound to come out during the trial that the gang came here precisely because you would provide them with a cover, and that things were being replaced *after* you had catalogued them.'

'That will be very hard to prove, and in any case proof probably won't be much help. I'll still be a laughing stock for living amongst reproductions and not even spotting them. In any case the damage will already have been done by all the rumours that will have been circulating.'

Rumours! When would we see an end to them and the harm they could do? Just then Helena appeared, coming from the house with Cleopatra and Claudia Crespi. I was surprised, to say the least, to see how radiant — exultant, even — Helena looked, given the circumstances. Spotting us she made a beeline for Mark, as he visibly shrank back.

'My dear, dear fellow!' Helena said, taking him by the hand. 'Where have you been? We must continue the cataloguing! I am most anxious to have it finished in time for the trial.'

'But . . .' began Mark.

'Yes, *caro*, you must go now and finish your work. We can talk later over a drink, no?'

'Now do let's go and talk over what's left to be done,' Helena continued, leading Mark off looking dazed and dream-like.

'Good Lord!' I said. 'What on earth has happened?'

'Ah, you have not heard, obviously. Word has come that the English Big House Wedding Heaven was mysteriously burnt down last night.'

'But surely that's dreadful!' said Cathy. 'The evidence has been destroyed!'

'Ah, no,' Claudia explained. 'There is much left of the Scottish castle, and also of the Cotswold cottage. But as for the things that were taken from here – that were *thought* to have been taken, I mean –'

'*What*?' I exclaimed.

'Yes, yes; you must understand that nothing had yet been stolen,' said Claudia, looking rather Sphynx-like. 'You see, nothing pertaining to this Abbey has survived the fire. Look at it this way. Helena has now an organ of the first quality, hand-made, that plays beautifully. She has panelling with no rot, and beams with no worm holes, and wonderful furniture of the finest wood. Soon my *Marchetto* will identify all the other good things that she now has. Of course, if asked in court he will have to say that he was unaware of any reproductions being introduced into the Abbey. So, what would you do? Helena has made up her mind that nothing has been stolen.'

'But it's not *true*.' said Cathy, to which Claudia replied with a Mediterranean shrug of her shoulders.

'How do you know?' she asked. 'Are you an expert? And anyway, why shouldn't Helena have some luck? Who does it harm? The thief will be convicted of the theft of the other things, and for murder.'

Well, I never!' I began, but Cathy got in first.

'What I don't understand is why he went to all that trouble to replace and export all that rotten old stuff. Why not have it copied, and keep the copies himself?'

she asked. I thought it best not to allude to my previous conversation with Helena.

'Ah, well, it seems that it is the rot and the worm holes that are valued in the Orient as being particularly authentic,' Claudia said.

'Well, be that as it may, why put proper workings into our organ, and take the broken stuff?' Cathy asked.

'But it seems that he did not take the insides of the organ. Indeed he was not interested in them. They have been found buried on the bog in a box. Not knowing that the organ didn't work, he had a reproduction made that does work. But the old one he wanted only for the outside. It was to be given an electronic inside.'

'Well,' said Cathy, 'that's too improbable sounding to be believed by a jury. I think that they are most likely to believe that nothing was taken in the first place, especially since Mark didn't notice anything. Oh, well, I suppose it's for the best, really.'

'Of course it is!' said Claudia. My poor *Marco* has suffered enough already, and Helena deserves some free renovations. *E' tutto perfetto.*'

It was all most irregular, but it seemed at that time to be all we could do. The long, drawn out *dénouement* of the trial, the evidence and the eventual acknowledgement of the reproductions (which make it possible to include this conversation in my narrative) would make a book in itself, and is without my remit. I will thus restrict the conclusion of my narrative to tying up a few loose ends related our homicidal mystery.

20
Loose Ends

High summer had come at last, and with it warm, sunny days. But the evenings were already shortening with the intimation of the coming autumn. It was hard to think that soon it would be a year since Michael's body was found, and our drama began to unfold. Lucy was home from hospital, not fully recovered of course, but convalescing. Steve had hired both a night and a day nurse, insisting on having her at home as soon as possible. 'I'm not having her around all that noise and dirt,' he had said. 'She'll just end up catching lots of super bugs. Besides, we've got a great clinic just up the road.' And that of course is the case. I had developed the habit of helping Steve at the yard, as well as coming up to the Blackmores' house for an hour or so in the evening to read the sporting pages to Lucy, and to have some banter with Alice. It is so easy to intrude upon a family at this sort of time, especially when there is no mother in the house; so I was very alive to any sense that I might overstay my welcome. But Steve had put my mind at rest. 'It helps to make the house seem more normal,' he had said. 'Alice is taking it all particularly hard. I think it all reminds her of . . .' and here I had put a hand on his arm to spare him continuing.

On one particular evening, I made my way up their drive bearing a special gift. Angela Carrington had discovered that Alice was very fond of lasagna, and had made her secret recipe for *lasagna al forno* specially. I had been detailed to bring it up together with Angela's own *pane rustico*, an *insalata verde*, and a bottle of the still ubiquitous Santa Maria degli Angeli *prosecco* (*not* for Alice!). I hallooed as I opened the kitchen door bearing my gifts, and there I was met by a pleasant surprise. Lucy was sitting by the Aga, wrapped up in an armchair.

'Well, this really is a celebration!' I said 'Where's your father? I'll just pop the lasagna in the oven for you to keep it warm.'

'Oh, lasagna, lasagna! I love lasagna. Mummy used to make us lasagna,' sang Alice, hopping around the kitchen. Lucy looked as if she were about to try to speak, which she was to be careful of. Alice prevented her, saying, 'Daddy's just coming down. He said we were going to have a party because of Lucy being able to come down, and because of the lasagna.' And indeed, I saw the kitchen table already set for four.

'Are you having someone to supper?' I asked.

'Of course,' said Steve coming in. 'You're staying, aren't you? I can't drink that all myself,' said, indicating the wine. 'And Lucy's not allowed to.'

'Oh, Dad,' Lucy said weakly.

'No, not yet. Doctor's orders. And when you *are* allowed, I've got a very nice bottle of champagne waiting for you.'

And so, I found myself serving supper, and then sitting among them all in the warmth of their home. It reminded me suddenly of my own family home, which had evaporated years and years before with the deaths of my own parents. When Steve sat down and said, 'Lord, bless this food, and all who eat it. Amen.' I couldn't help adding to myself, "God bless us, every one!"

It was not long after that evening that Cathy and I were invited for another special treat. Claudia had informed us that *Newsnight Review* that week was to feature the prestigious new Gulbenkian/Finkelstein contemporary sculpture awards, direct from the Metropolitan Art Museum in New York. She had invited Penny, Cathy, and me to her flat to watch it together with herself and Mark, in the hope that Debbie might have won something. I therefore went to call on Cathy in good time, and we started out to walk over together. 'Isn't that curious about Max,' I asked as we came down the stairs of her apartment.

'Max at the farm?' she asked, startled. 'Why, what's happened?'

I detected an anxious air about her voice, so I hastened to say, 'Oh, nothing the matter, quite the opposite. It transpires that he had got in with some gambling ring. He decided to talk to Helena about it, and she advised him to speak to the Guards, and you'll never guess what happened!'

'What?' Cathy asked rather worriedly.

'Well, the others, to whom Max claimed to owe money, categorically denied any knowledge of it! And on top of that, they've threatened him with legal action for slander if he says any more about it! So, of course, he can't say who they were. But more importantly, he doesn't have to pay his gambling debts, which I gather were considerable.' After the confrontation with Debbie about using the van, Max had indeed realised that by remaining silent he was leaving himself open to blackmail later. He had been reluctant to tell Judy that he had spoken to the Guards, but as it transpired, she was very relieved that he had done so. Secrets like that are a perpetual burden.

'Oh, good man!' cried Cathy happily. 'I'm so happy for them both.' And so it was that Cathy was able to unburden herself at last of the confidence Judy had placed in her. It was therefore with rather a celebratory feeling that we arrived at Claudia's flat, now almost bare from her packing.

'*Ciao, ciao*,' she said, showing us in. 'We will have an *aperitivo*, yes? Marco is already here, and Penny.' And indeed, there on a table were plates of the delightful *hors d'œuvres* without which no Italian cocktail party is complete. Accepting glasses of *prosecco*, we looked about at the now meagrely furnished room.

'It looks so sad being so empty,' Cathy said, voicing my thoughts. 'I'm so glad that you're not actually leaving us.'

'Oh, but no!' said Claudia. 'After the wedding we will have a little time in *Sardegna*, and then we come back to our own house here.'

'You're buying here, are you?' I asked Mark. 'How will that tie in with your work?'

THE SERPENT IN THE GARDEN

'Ah, you obviously haven't heard,' he answered. 'I've decided to go in with Sinead Slattery on her antiques shop. And I can do consultancy work no matter where I'm based. Sinead really doesn't want to take the boys away from their friends, but she can't be everywhere at once. It will suit us both very well. She's really silver and jewelry anyway.'

'How delightful!' exclaimed Cathy. 'And have you actually found a house already?'

'Yes, a lovely house, in Drum. The view is magnificent, isn't it *caro*?' said Claudia turning to Mark.

'But what about your own work?' I asked Claudia. 'There can't be much in Ireland for a herpetologist to do, apart from newts.'

'Ah, newts!' said Claudia with a dismissive wave of her hand. 'I am tired of amphibians. But soon I will go to Burren and study the slow worms.'

'Are there many in Ireland?' asked Cathy.

'It is this that I will find out!' said Claudia with determination.

'But what about funding?' I asked. 'You can't earn a living writing about slow worms. Surely you will want to have a university appointment here.'

'University appointments! Why should I want to work anymore for universities? Wasting time on bored students, writing about silly things because the university says, "We want so many articles on this and so many on that". This way, I can study what I like and write what I like. Marco is an authority, and his business will do well. I can live a good life, and cook, and make a nice house.

And besides, Angela and I are starting our own little business. We are going to import some very nice things from my home, and either find outlets for them or sell them to special friends. That would be more fun.'

I must confess that listening to Claudia speak, I couldn't help but be aware of the force of her argument. All too soon the term of my readership would expire and I would be back to the old grind of commuting and teaching, and writing articles about 'silly things.' I had so much enjoyed my scholarly freedom of the last three years (murder and mayhem notwithstanding), that I knew it would be a wrench to return to student records and funding applications. My *magnum opus*, the product of my readership and its remit, was even now at press. *Pythagorean Ratios in the Alexandrian Christian Tradition* had been enormous fun to write and, given the choice, I would much have preferred continuing the subject into an examination of the influence of Christian Platonic geometry on Byzantine aesthetics, particularly iconography. But instead all I had to look forward to was endless Augustine, and his dreary Latin progeny.

I was soon shaken from these reflections though by the clock; it was time for *Newsnight Review*. We all gathered round the television as Martha Kearney outlined the contents of the evening's programme. And there, live from New York, was Kirsty Warke, whose report on the International Contemporary Sculpture Exhibition at the Metropolitan Museum of Art would occupy most of it. An exited murmur arose among us. It seemed incredible to think that there in the vast hall behind Kirsty, one of us had a competition piece on display. 'Cross your fingers, everyone,' said Claudia excitedly, and I found myself holding my breath. The report commenced with an overview of the exhibition, and its various categories. Figurative sculpture formed only a part of it, and most of that seemed to be in the bulky Henry Moore tradition.

'I can't believe that people are still doing that chunky stuff,' observed Cathy. 'It's so *old*.'

'Oh, look look look! Oh you missed it,' cried Claudia. 'It was Debbie's piece; I saw it. There look!' And sure enough, the camera moved back towards an elegant bronze figure of a kneeling woman, about half life size. We all recognised it as Debbie's more 'classical' style, and then the caption came up '*Pietà*, Deborah English'.

'There's something on the plinth; she's won something,' said Mark.

'Why won't they give us a closer look?' asked Penny.

'She's still describing the exhibition,' I said.

'Shh! She's explaining the prizes!' hissed Claudia.

Here followed a full, and for us frustrating explanation of the patrons' purpose in establishing the exhibition, which was intended to take place every five years. Then at last the categories for awards, and finally we were shown the winning pieces. Figures were, of course, the last category to be covered, and when the award winner was shown we all let out a groan of disappointment. 'Another chunky thing,' Cathy said with exasperation.

'Shh, wait wait,' said Claudia. And indeed Kirsty was explaining that, due to the difficulty of judging between abstract and representational sculpture, it had been decided to make a subsidiary award for whichever sort hadn't won the overall figure prize. And there it was; we all gasped as, at last, Debbie's figure was shown close up.

'How exquisite,' said Cathy. For my part, I would have said that Debbie had achieved a finely poised balance between abstract and representational. The dead Christ, rather than being shown on Mary's lap, as is traditional, was obviously meant to be lying in front of her kneeling figure. His form was very simply suggested by the folds of some drapery. Mary herself seemed to have been caught in the act of raising her arms to heaven. Their outstretched curve formed not a static arc, but seemed to have been conceived along the lines of a logarithmic curve (something dear to my heart), the right arm straighter and higher than the left. The classical pose of the figure was however balanced by an extreme economy of technique. Planes and contours were suggested in the drapery, rather than executed in detail. Somehow the composition seemed both perfectly academic, and radically mobile. But our admiration reached its zenith when the camera gave us a close up of the head. Instead of being covered, it was bare, Mary's hair flowing about her shoulders. And in the midst of it, with an expression that blended both the agony of grief and the joy of hope, was the face of Claudia Crespi.

'It's you!' cried Mark, as stupefied as the rest of us.

'So that was the "surprise" you were planning with Debbie!' I said.

'Shh! She's still talking about it,' said Claudia. But the report soon moved to other parts of the exhibition.

'Oh how frustrating! Do you think they'll come back to it?' asked Cathy.

'Should we watch the rest of the programme in case?' asked Penny.

'Why not just turn the sound down, and if we see it again we can turn it up,' I suggested.

'Good idea,' said Mark, who then turned to Claudia and demanded, 'What's all this about?'

'I'm sorry, *caro*. Debbie didn't want anyone to know anything at all about the figure until after the awards. If she hadn't won anything, I would have waited until the wedding. But now, since you have all seen it, I might as well give you this early.' And so saying, Claudia went to a cupboard, and lifted out what was obviously a heavy box, somewhat larger than a shoebox. 'This is my wedding present,' she said as she handed it to Mark. You may well imagine that we crowded round as he opened it, notwithstanding the fact that it was a very private gift. He opened the lid, and then set on the table a perfect miniature copy of the award-winning sculpture. 'That was her payment to me for modelling,' said Claudia. 'I had only to pay for the bronze and the casting.'

'There it is again!' said Penny, and we turned to see the original on the television as the credits rolled.

'What a wonderful day,' said Cathy as Claudia turned off the television. 'Everything seems to be working out wonderfully for everyone.'

'Except Dickie,' said Penny, 'and Michael.'

We all sat in silence a moment, sobered. 'Well,' I said at last, rallying, 'Dickie knew perfectly well that he was involved in something criminal. He was old enough to know that there is no honour among thieves.'

'And Michael?' asked Cathy.

'Well, I gather that Moto killed him because he was snooping and prying about. He might have been trying a spot of blackmail. Or else Moto just got irritated with him.'

'I should think that was it,' said Cathy. 'He certainly was irritating, poor chap.'

It had been a lovely party, but we all realised that Claudia and Mark would want to be alone. So we took our leave, and having said goodnight to Penny, Cathy and I decided to have a chat about everything at my flat over a nightcap. As we sat drinking our Irish cocoa (a speciality of mine), Theophrastes curled up by the fire, Cathy coughed gently in preparation for broaching what she obviously considered to be a delicate subject. As we have been friends from childhood she knows she can speak frankly to me, even on personal matters.

'You know Robbie, I always wondered why you never married. It's never too late, you know.'

'Heavens', I replied, 'I'm well past having children.'

'It isn't just about that, as you know very well. Companionship is the main thing; that's still there after the children have flown the nest. I think you know that there is someone who would like to be your very good companion, if you were interested; and I think that person could make you very happy.'

I sighed. 'I have to be honest with you, dear Cathy. Every man I have ever fancied has turned out to be a scoundrel. I seem always to have had an unerring instinct for choosing a rotten egg. When I look back at some of the young fellows who turned my head, and think what became of them subsequently, it makes my hair stand on end.'

'Ah', said Cathy, sagely. 'I always wondered whether you and Dickie . . .'

Reader, I blushed. So much for thirty years of well-kept secret, as I had thought! Rallying from my confusion, I said, 'Yes, well; as I have said, in my girlhood I might have been employed by the Guards as a litmus test for whether a fellow was a wrong 'un. As for Dickie, look what he came to! Imagine if I had been married to him! Imagine if we had had children! Where would I be now?'

'Ah, but if you had married him, he might never have come to a sticky end.'

'I very much object,' I said, 'to that school of thought in which it is believed to be a woman's purpose to save men from themselves. I am more concerned about what a dance I might have been led in the attempt. No, my dear. I confess that I have also considered the possibility that I believe you are suggesting; I forbear to name the individual I think we both have in mind. I admit that I have a soft spot for him. But I am really too old now for new adventures, and quite set in my ways. I am very comfortably settled, and I don't intend to spoil that. Theophrastes and I get on very well as we are, don't we precious?'

To which Theophrastes responded with an emphatic 'Miaow!'